SONG TITLE SERIES

THE RAT PACK

Featuring

Frank Sinatra

Dean Martin

Sammy Davis Jr.

JOAN MAGUIRE

Copyright Page

New: The Rat Pack
Author: Joan Maguire

National Library of Australia Cataloguing-in-Publication – Publication entry

Creator:	Maguire, Joan, author
Title:	The Rat Pack/ Joan Maguire.
Edition:	Large print edition
ISBN:	9780994329769 (paperback)
Series:	Song title series (large print); book 11.
Notes:	Includes bibliography references
Subjects	Families --Fiction
	Titles of musical compositions--Fiction
Dewey Number:	A823. 4

Published with the assistance of CreateSpace and is available through the Print on Demand Network or www.songtitleseries.com

This short story book was created and written
By Joan Maguire on 24th July 2013 ©
ISBN: 978-0-9941998-2-9
E-book re-written April 2014©
EIBSN: 978-0-9925964-7-7
This book was converted into large print in March 2015©
and is available through the same distributors as the normal book or www.songtitleseries.com.
ISBN 978-0-9943297-6-9 (large print)

DEDICATION

I would like to dedicate this book and to say thank you to my Earth Angel David and his friends, who inspire and motivate me to achieve things that I never dreamt, were possible.

INTRODUCTION

Legally I cannot use Lyrics or Music because of Copyright but I can use song titles so a total of 1337 song titles (Italicized) have been used and due to the nature of my books; legally I must place a Reference (exactly as it is down loaded) and Bibliography after the story.

Fred and Sylvia Dawson married and raised their four children in the suburb of Monologue just across the river from New York.

Nancy, the eldest, has decided to have a family reunion at her place in Chicago at Christmas time and it turns out to be more than a family gathering as each person reveals a hidden secret.

Can Sam, their youngest daughter's husband shed light on this mystery by telling them a story from his Peruvian ancestry.

Does his story have anything to do with the certain person that has visited his other relatives and the UFO sightings?

ACKNOWLEDGEMENTS

I would like to thank my daughters, Jenny and Kylie for their positive but critical input in the first draft of this book and all the help and support that they have given me throughout the Song Title Series books. With taking their input to mind, I have improved the book.

I would also like to thank my son Peter and his family for their support and help in keeping me grounded.

I would like to thank Kay and Julie for their patience and understanding whilst teaching me and giving me the skills to present my unique books in the best way possible.

I would also like to thank everyone else who has helped me bring this book to life and to you for purchasing it.

IN NEW YORK

It started as *a foggy day,* on one of the last days of *autumn in New York.* Sylvia and Fred Dawson had decided to catch *the Hucklebuck* tram into the big city to complete their Christmas shopping. *The Hucklebuck* tram was mainly used around Christmas time to commute the citizens of their community of *Monologue* across the river to down town New York.

Normally people would take a leisurely walk across the bridge that crossed the river, *as that lucky old sun* would shine down on them; but at this time of year, *the river's too wide* to cross in the cold and *stormy weather.*

Come sundown, the *smoke, smoke, smoke* from the chimneys of the large opulent houses; not to mention *a mansion* or two that the *folks who live on a hill* lived in, would start filling the air as they started burning their log fires, which meant that it would be a *lovely way to spend an evening;* warm and cosy.

Over the years the *smoke, smoke,*

smoke had decreased as the introduction of central heating was accessed by many home owners.

Across the road from their home was the *Monologue* Park that many people enjoyed visiting, especially under the *blue skies* and warm weather of a spring or summer day.

As the seasons changed and the weather became colder, many species of birds would sing their *September song* and fly south to the warmer climate. Some smaller children would often say "*Bye, bye blackbird,* I'll see you next year."

There was also a pond that froze over in the winter months and many people would spend a leisurely *Saturday night* skating on it. On the odd occasion, you could hear *Hey there,* Dave, are you going to that new *Birth Of The Blues* Club when you leave here? or *Hey won't you play* tag with me? or *Let me go lover* before we both fall over, or *Baby, it's cold outside* coming from the park and pond.

There was also a coffee vendor that

used to play a *Coffee Song* as he approached the park so that the *guys and dolls* could buy hot coffee, chocolate or *tea for two* and *candy kisses* cakes or biscuits in the shape of a *spinning wheel* from him.

Some evenings; especially during the warmer months, Sylvia and Fred would sit on their front veranda and reminisce about their youth, early married life and the four children that they had raised in their house.

One recent evening Sylvia said "I remember the first time that we went skating over there. My parents had moved here only three months before hand and *I left my heart in San Francisco* with my friends. That day, *I got the sun in the morning* in my bedroom that woke me up and I wasn't very happy about that. I had also made arrangements to meet some people and go skating with them *just for fun.*

One of the guys that was with the group started to get too friendly so I said to him "*Hit the road Jack, can't you see*

I've got the blues. Me and my shadow want to be left alone thank you."

Then I saw you with a couple of your mates walking *on the sunny side of the street* towards the park and suddenly, the "*Oh, lonesome me"* attitude disappeared and the "*I ain't got nobody"* thought changed.

All of me wanted to get to know *all of you*. It was a couple of days later when I was out *on an evening with Roma* and Kelly at *That's Amore* that we bumped into each other and we sat talking. That was the time that I knew that *I only have eyes for you* and no-one else."

"Yes, I remember that evening." said Fred "I was *once in love with Amy;* well, I thought I was and *I confess* that *I fall in love to easily,* so I made arrangements with Kelly to take you out *on an evening with Roma* and her to the *That's Amore* Café and that we would meet up there.

All of me wanted to get to know *all of you* as well, so instead of letting *fools rush in,* or should I say, a fool rush in and find that I've made another mistake; I made sure that we were there with friends and that we could quite easily leave with them.

I had seen you as I was walking *on the sunny side of the street* with my mates and *my heart stood still* as I thought "*How cute can you be* and at this moment *I ain't got nobody,* so why not try to get to know her, even though *I don't stand a ghost of a chance* of doing so."

After the meeting at *That's Amore,* I knew then that *I've got you under my skin* and *I've got you under my skin* still. Usually *money burns a hole in my pocket,* but *because of you,* I wanted to save it so that I could send you a *room full of roses* every day."

Sylvia went on saying "I never had to look forward to the *same old Saturday night* again and when I received *my funny Valentine* Day card, I knew that *if I ever love again* that it would be with you.

I did have a special young man back home and that is why I always said that *I left my heart in San Francisco;* however, when I met you I had to ask myself a few times over "*Which way did my heart go* and *what is this thing called love?*

What kind of fool am I or would be if I let *someone like you* go out of my life. *If I loved you;* I knew for sure that *somebody loves me* and I knew that *I've got a crush on you* so I thought *taking a chance on love* with you would be the right thing to do and it was.

Love; marriage, four beautiful and successful children, ten wonderful grandchildren and a husband that I still love and adore and who will hold me whenever he feels like it; whether I need it or not, is all I need."

Fred looked at his wife and *tenderly* said "After all these years *it never entered my mind* that when you moved here with your parents, you left a boyfriend behind, and you have never mentioned it. I knew that you would either *love me or leave me* and that I would have it *all or nothing at all.*

My heart stood still at the time when you told me that you were going back to San Francisco for a while. I thought "*Here comes the blues* again and just after *you brought a new kind of love to me. Everybody loves somebody* and if you loved me and *if I loved you* enough, then you would come back to me."

You left and I heard nothing from you and I often thought of you *night and day* and sometimes I would think "*I wonder who's kissing her now?"*

Two months later you returned and when we met, the first thing you said to me was "*Hold me,* you *embraceable you. I knew that you'd be so nice to come home to."*

It was then that I knew that *the girl that I marry* was going to be you. You were *my kind of girl* in *my kind of town* and you didn't have to worry whether you could *get me to the church on time* because I was there early waiting for you.

That day I promised "All my love is *dedicated to you* and *everything I have is yours* and *I'll always love you."*

What made you think of our first

meeting now after all these happy years?"

Sylvia's reply was "*I'll always love you* too. I was looking at our garden and I noticed just how many rose bushes we have and that made me think back to when you said that you wanted to give me a *room full of roses* every day.

Well my dear, I think that you have done more than that for me; even though I love you deeply; *I've got a crush on you* still, *I've got you under my skin* even more than before, and still *I only have eyes for you.*

Yes; *we could have been the closest of friends* but I think that we are the best friend that either of us could have. *You and I* have been through a lot together; good, bad and funny. You told me once that I'll always have *someone to watch over me* and I have.

Can you remember that time before we got married that I went away on holidays. Well; I met my old boyfriend back home and because *I love Vegas,* he took me there.

One night he left me standing near the slot machines while he went off to play poker, or so he said, and I suddenly saw the reflection of a very handsome man with a beautiful smile and sensuous blue eyes standing behind me, in one.

I tried to turn around but I was frozen on the spot and he said to me "*You'll never walk alone* and if you go back to the park, *you're gonna love yourself* even more on your return, because *here lies love* and *memories are made of this* and many more *beautiful things* and happenings in your life.

If you *powder your face with sunshine* every morning, you will always be *young at heart.* Life is like a dance, you *begin the beguine* and before long you find out that it *takes two to tango.*

You will never live on the *street of dreams* because your dreams will always come true. If you look *east of the sun, west of the moon* on *a foggy day* you will find *my shining hour.*

On the sunny side of the street is where you will always live until *the day after forever.* Life is so unpredictable, yep, life, *she's funny that way.*"

My old boyfriend came back to me and I noticed that he had lipstick still on the side of his lip.

He said "*Hey there,* I will have to take you back to your hotel early as I have to go over to the *Blue Smoke* Hotel and find the manager Mr. *Vieni Su* because *I left my hat in Haiti* Gong's kitchen while we were *makin' Whoopee* this afternoon.

Making Whoopee; his new cocktail is made by squeezing the limes and oranges for their juice, and that is what I was doing while he was mixing the alcohols and then he mixed both the fruit juice and alcohol together in a shaker with ice."

I thought *now it lies, now it lies, now it lies;* he is off to meet another female and *you're breaking my heart all over again* and that's when I started *thinking of you* and *the nearness of you* made me realize that although *I can't give you anything but love, you make me feel so young* and you will always be honest with me and be there for me.

Just as we were leaving the games room I heard in my head "*Don't forget tonight tomorrow* and *try a little tenderness.*"

There were a few moments of silence between the couple as Fred looked over his garden and thought "*Should I* tell Sylvia that about the same time as her encounter with that man, I also had an encounter with a similar looking man.

I remember he told me "*Something's gotta give* and *in the cool, cool, cool of the evening* something will give and that will change your life in a good way forever.

If *fools rush in* to love and find that they have made a mistake; then this time you are no fool for you will not make a mistake.

Have a little sympathy and *try a little tenderness* in the beginning and your love will be colored with *polka dots and moonbeams* and *out of this world* with happiness.

I always say that life is so unpredictable. Yep; life, *she's funny that way,* but the saying that *you're nobody till somebody loves you* is not true, because somebody will see something in you, that will attract you to them.

It could be *when you're smiling,* so *smile darn ya smile,* or in your *devil may care,* happy-go-lucky attitude. You will be lucky but will that *luck be a lady* that will make you feel like the *king of the road* or something else?

It's a lovely day tomorrow and that's when you will find out. *Somewhere along the way* you will mention me to others but until that time comes, and you will know when the time is, *please don't talk about me when I'm gone."* No, I don't think this is the right time."

Albert looked at Sylvia and said "I'm going to put the kettle on. Shall I make *tea for two?"*

This year, Christmas was being held at their eldest daughter, *Nancy*'s place in *Chicago* and it was also going to be a big family reunion for them, so there were extra presents to buy.

They were looking forward to being with their other three children and their seven grandchildren, who either lived overseas or in Canada; but what gifts to buy each of them was a difficult decision.

Sylvia knew that her granddaughter, *Louise* was an avid reader, so they were going to a great little book shop just over *the Brooklyn Bridge* to buy her some books and they could also have morning tea *at The Salad Bar* next to the book shop.

She also knew that the two youngest granddaughters were still toddlers, so a small moving toy would entertain them for a short time.

Yesterday, Sylvia and Fred had sat down at their kitchen table and began writing a shopping list. First of all, they wrote down the names in each family, in order of age starting with their parents.

They then wrote the suggested gift items beside each person that had been given to them and where they might be able to purchase the gift.

If they were unsure of what to buy, they were going to get their daughter to take them shopping once they were in *Chicago*.

Fred said "We had better make all of Frank's family's presents small because they will have to take it back with them. I think that when their business trip to London has finished, they are flying to *Chicago* before flying home to Canada after Christmas, so they will have enough to carry as it is."

"I suppose you're right, we should make all the gifts small so they will be easier for them all to take home." said Sylvia "It was suggested that we buy John a music box set of *Just The Hits;* however, Frank didn't tell us which band or singer that John listens to, and so I think that one will be a *Chicago* purchase.

Now; *what I've got in mind* for *sweet Lorraine* and Stella is, *the glow worm* that wriggles when you stroke it. What do you think or have you any other ideas for them?"

"I thought that the *Kiddie Album*

medley would have been alright for them, but thinking about it now, *the glow worm* would be better. The *Kiddie Album medley* would be too old for them now, but we could always send it to them for their next birthdays.

I saw in the Macy's toy booklet that they have a *King Of The Road* four wheel drive that pulls a *caravan,* on sale for half the normal price. We could get that for Shannon; you know how sometimes he pretended to be the *Wichita lineman* who travelled to *far away places* and down the *Lonesome Road* that stretched across the desert." said Fred.

"Fred, *be honest with me* now. Do you think that a boy of *eee-o-eleven* would still play with toys like that?

He would be more into those *Ghost Riders In The Sky* games that they can play on their computers at home?" asked Sylvia "and because Shannon, Dean, Romeo and Antonio are all in that nine to eleven age bracket; why don't we go out and buy eight of those games and give them to the boys for Christmas.

We could get them to open them up
and *if* they had that particular game, they
could swap with one of the others *if* they
wanted to. I think that Wal-Mart had
those games advertised this week."

Fred grabbed the booklet from off the
bench and looked through it until he
came to the second last page and then
he said "You're right. They have *That Old
Black Magic,* The *Birth Of The Blues*
Gang, *De Camptown Races* Heist, *Ghost
Riders In The Sky, Long Ago And Far
Away* Space Invaders, *Who's Sorry Now*
Western, Now *Who's Got The Action* and
Wogon Wheels Rodeo.

If we plan and get to Wal-Mart early,
then we should be able to buy one of
each and that would be most of our
Christmas shopping done in one hit; also
they would be easy for us to pack and
take on the plane.

We could go to the Wal-Mart that's
opposite the book shop that we want to
go to. Now; all we have to do is think of
something for Frank's two children and
our other two granddaughters."

Sylvia said "Don't forget our own children; they get presents as well. I was thinking that maybe one evening whilst we are there, we could baby-sit and send *Nancy* and Bob off to have a meal and see the *Dean's Vegas Melody* Cabaret Show at the *Impressions* Hotel.

Nancy mentioned that she would like to go and see it but being Christmas, her normal sitter was unavailable.

I was thinking that I would wait until we went shopping in *Chicago* to get *Frankie and Johnnie,* Rose and Sam's presents. Our little *ramblin' Rose* was always hard to shop for."

"That she was." said Fred "I remember when she was a little girl and she used to tell me "I have *the gypsy in my soul"* but I never realized how true it was until she turned eighteen and started to travel.

She told me one day when she was about sixteen that "Most people live in a *marshmallow world* and try to live *the impossible dream*. Many of my friends are *young & foolish* because *they say it's wonderful* to be in love and they do all *these foolish things just for fun.*

Then a few months later some of them come crying to me asking, "What do you do *when your lover has gone?"*

Time after time fools rush in to relationships, looking for *just one more chance* to be happy because they think that *you're nobody till somebody loves you.*

Look at me; I'm somebody and I'm happy because *everybody loves somebody* to love them and my family loves me. I've *a lot of livin' to do* besides *I'm gonna live until I die* or until *love and marriage* ties me down; even then I'll be saying *let's keep swinging* down that road of life."

She has done a lot since she has started travelling but *love & marriage* and two children still haven't slowed her down."

"Well, my dear. What would you like for Christmas? and don't say that all I need is you because *I've got my love to keep me warm* in winter when you *hold me* and *you make me feel so young* during summer like you always say when I ask you similar questions." said Sylvia.

"I was looking at some new gardening tools but *I got a great big shovel* and my other tools are still pretty new. Next spring I'm going to plant an *American Beauty Rose* near the violets and I hope that we get many *violets for your furs* next year.

I will have to cut back that *Muskat Ramble* vine because it's taking over the place. I might even get rid of it altogether and put another *American Beauty Rose* in its place. I would have to see what colors that they come in before I make any real decisions.

Another idea would be some new books. I wouldn't mind those new detective story books "*Crap Game In New York* and *Crap Game In New York and Macarthur Park.*

Other than that I don't really know what I want. And what would you like for Christmas my dear?" asked Fred.

"*Peace on earth* but I know that will not happen in my life time.

A few extra *pennies from heaven* wouldn't go astray.

Seriously, *there are things* I would like to have but don't really need; but having my family around is so much more important to me.

As *rambling Rose* said "*Everybody loves somebody*" and I love you more than anyone *because you're mine*.

You met *June in January* while she was on holidays here from Australia and when she went back, *the sky fell down* on you for a short while but you knew *this can't be love* that you were feeling for her so you started going out with your mates again and that's when we met.

I use to love it when we went to *The Continental* Ballroom and afterwards when you used to suggest quite adamantly "*Let's take an old fashioned walk*" *in the wee small hours of the morning*.

You knew that I would be in some sort of trouble with my father for being out so late; but that didn't stop you, and you knew just how to get around my father and smooth things over until the next time. In the end my father gave up getting mad with me.

I still remember the look on your face and the fear in your eyes after you proposed to me.

I think it went like this "*A fellow needs a girl* to be with for the rest of his life but *I can't give you anything but love,* so will you marry me anyway and *love me as I am.*"

When I said yes, you jump and cheered from the East Thirty First Street *corner to corner* of *Memory Lane* where you wanted to go *swinging down the lane* with me. You gave *the naughty lady of Shady Lane* a hug, and you had me *dancing with tears in my eyes* because I was so happy.

You became very quiet and reserved once we reached my front door because it hit you, that although I had said yes, you still had to ask my parents; especially my father." said Sylvia.

"Yes, I remember that night. I didn't know if *this is the beginning of the end* of our romance and I worried right the way *through a long sleepless night* until I spoke to your father the following day.

Now shouldn't we get ready and get started for the day. While we're out and about, we might see something for the others that we need to buy for." said Fred, trying to get away from the subject that his wife had just brought up.

Sylvia looked at the clock and said "*If we leave here in ten minutes*, we can get the new tram that will take us directly over the bridge to Wal-Mart and that will mean that we won't have change trams or walk over the bridge from the city. These days, I'm finding that *the river's too wide* for me to walk over."

Fred looked out of the lounge window to see *that lucky old sun* breaking through the clearing fog and called out to his wife "Sylvia, I think that you should put your thick woollen coat on 'cos *baby it's cold outside*. I know that you most probably won't need it in the stores but we won't be spending all day in the stores; well, I hope not."

As they were travelling on the tram, Fred and Sylvia still discussed ideas for the Christmas presents that they still had to find and buy.

On the tram and out of the blue, Fred looked at Sylvia and said "I still can't believe *you're mine, you* wonderful woman. To me, *you are too beautiful* still. I think that it's *you and your beautiful eyes, the sunshine of your smile* and the way that you *powder your face with sunshine* every day that makes you beautiful and not to mention your honest and caring heart." and then he turned his head and glanced out of the tram window for a second before turning back to her.

"Why, thank you." she said "and what made you tell me that now?"

"*I don't know why.* Do I have to have a reason to tell you how I feel?" asked Fred.

"No, but of *all the things you are,* you are not so romantic when we are out in public. Here is our stop, so where do you think that we should go first?" replied Sylvia.

"I think that we should go to Wal-Mart first and then if it's time, we could have some lunch *at The Salad Bar* and then go to the bookshop before heading home." said Fred.

"That's *what I've got in mind* to do as well but if we finish there early enough, I was thinking that we could pop into Macys before heading home." replied Sylvia.

They headed straight for the games section and were lucky to get the last games in store of *That Old Black Magic,* The *Birth Of The Blues* Gang, *Ghost Riders In the Sky,* and *Who's Sorry Now* Western.

Fred noticed that there were plenty of the other games, like *You Go To My Head* Puzzles and *One For My Baby* Girl Game that were left and remarked to Sylvia that they couldn't be as popular and wondered if they should buy them.

Sylvia said "They may not be popular at the moment but it doesn't mean that our grandsons won't like to play them.

I think that the *One For My Baby* Girl

Game would be meant for young girls to play because they wouldn't be interested in the sort of games that boys like to play. Now, I think that it's too early for lunch but a spot of *tea for two* would be nice, don't you think so?"

Over in the book shop, Sylvia noticed a book with the title "*I Get A Kick Out Of You*" which was a joke book and then she noticed another book called "*The Oldest Established Permanent Floating Crap Game In New York*" and wondered if it was like the other books that Fred was interested in getting.

She asked the assistant who told her that that was the original story and that the other two books were continuation stories. The assistant also told her that the copy they had was the last one and was very hard to find and that their store has been unsuccessful in trying to obtain more copies for the last six months.

Sylvia purchased the book without Fred noticing because he seemed to be engrossed in another book called "*On A Slow Boat To China*."

Sylvia startled Fred when she walked up beside him and said "You will have to buy it now or we will be back here every day so you can read some more. You can't start a story and then just leave it and you do have to have something to do when you're not able to get out in to the garden."

"It has started off as a good story and I would like to know how it ends. I know that you borrowed this book from the library last year and I didn't get a chance to read it so *please don't tell me how the story ends.*" Fred replied.

Fred carried his book and the games in a brown paper bag and there was still plenty of time for them to go and pick up a couple of items from Macys before heading home.

Come sundown, they were on the tram home that was packed with late shoppers and office workers. A couple of young men standing beside them were having a conversation about music and a new Club, The *Birth Of The Blues* Club, that they were going to go to that evening.

One of the men had reached his destination and was getting off the tram when the other young man called out "*Don't bring Lulu;* she won't fit in with the other *guys and dolls* that will be there. I'll call you later."

IN CHICAGO

In *Chicago, Nancy* and Bob were having the same discussion on what gifts to buy everyone. They had already purchased the gifts for their own children, Fred and Sylvia and John and Frank. They also knew what they were going to get for her other brother, Albert and his two sons but they had no ideas on what to get for her sister, Rose and her family.

They knew that Rose's husband Sam was a *nature boy;* well, he was when they had first met him but had he settled down since then. It was six years since they had last seen them.

The two of them stopped off in *Chicago* for a few days when they were on their way home from their holiday *on a slow boat to China.* Rose was pregnant at the time and couldn't get what she needed for the baby down near her home in Peru, so she decided to buy the baby supplies here and take them back with her.

Nancy pulled their last letter from Rose from the envelope and started to read the section that concerned their up and coming visit for Christmas.

If all went well and Sam returned on time from his next guided tour to Cusco, Sacred Valley and Machu Piccu, then they would fly out of Lima on the twenty second of December at eleven o'clock and would arrive in *Chicago* an hour later.

Rose had also written that they had completed all their Christmas shopping. *Nancy* had to smile to herself again when she read the part that Rose had written, after she had found out that all the family was staying under the same roof.

Rose had written "You didn't *mention a mansion*. I thought that you had a large two story house with a swimming pool and tennis court."

Bob and *Nancy* had renovated the underneath part of their house to make two guest rooms and a change room for the times that the pool was used. Their double garage that was attached to the house had also been made into a small unit for when their parents visited; which wasn't very often. They had worked out where everyone was sleeping except for Frank's two children.

They were both too old to sleep in the same room together or to share with any of their other cousins, so they had decided to hire a large caravan for them and put it next to the house where they would have access to both the house and the caravan through the laundry door.

They would both have their privacy but *Louise* would have the added security of her brother sleeping in a close proximity.

Extra beds were put in their own children's rooms, the boys would share one room, Christina would have Lorraine's room, Rose, Sam and Stella would sleep in Dean's Room. *Sweet Lorraine* would be sleeping in their room.

Just the thought of having four boys sharing one room scared her; but *Nancy* knew that it would only be for two weeks at the most and it would be worth it because she would be having her whole family together once more.

The other thing that had scared Nancy was the catering for all those extra people. Luckily, when she was first planning to have everyone there, she wrote and asked each one of her siblings for a couple of recipes of the foods they ate and if anyone had any special dietary requirements.

Nancy had received a few good simple recipes that could be made quite cheaply and would feed all the family so that made her grocery shopping a lot easier.

Rose and her family were vegetarians but Nancy could adapt the recipes to suit their meals. She knew that she would have enough help in preparing the meals and if they fed the younger children first, the adults could then sit and enjoy their meals in peace; or so she hoped.

They had hired a couple more tables and chairs so there would be enough seating inside. Being a *white Christmas* would make it impossible to eat outside because they had not enclosed their verandas from the cold.

With only five days to go before all of her siblings and her parents would arrive, Nancy checked her list to make sure that everything was in order.

Albert and Marie were flying in from Rome on the twenty first of December and Frank, Julie and Louise were flying in from London and would arrive at two pm on the twenty second of December whilst John was catching his flight from Paris and would be arriving an hour later than his parents. It seemed funny that Frank and the rest of his family and John were both leaving their destinations at the same time but John was landing an hour later.

Rose would also be arriving on the same day as Frank and John. Mom and dad were arriving mid-morning on the same day as Albert and his family; so she was happy with the knowledge that they only lived a half hour drive from the airport.

A terrible thought came to her head as she put the letter away. Would we still recognize each other?

The last time she had seen Albert was about nine years ago when he had come with his orchestra to the *San Fernando Valley* Music Festival that started off the *Birth Of The Blues* Festival, The Jazz Festival and the Classics Festival.

He had told them at the time, that *learnin' the blues* and jazz numbers seemed complicated but were fun. It also gave him a different direction to his music abilities. At that time he had told us that he was *in love* with one of the other musicians. *April played the fiddle* and violin and she was *five foot two, eyes of blue*.

Nancy remembered just how trim and tall he was and how a few months later, he wrote a letter telling her that *the one I love belongs to somebody else* and that April had got engaged to the *first Noel Figaro,* the grandson of *Luna Mezzo Mare. Luna Mezzo Mare* owned a chain of hotels and nightclubs; one being the *Mambo Italiano* Nightclub in Sigma Chi that Noel managed for his grandfather.

Noel had four brothers and three sisters

and one of his sisters, Maria, named her son Noel after her brother. To stop the confusion, *Maria* used to call her brother, the *first Noel* of the family or Noel senior.

Once April and Noel had married, she stopped playing music and helped her husband manage the *Mambo Italiano* Nightclub and she became known as *the sweetheart of Sigma Chi*.

Three months after that, Albert wrote saying that he was getting married to Marie *in Napoli* the following week. Marie was also *five foot two, eyes of blue* and she was a singer with the *Innamorata* Choir. I was rehearsing this *instrumental* piece and I looked up, just as *love walked in* to the room. Mr. Burbank was *introducing the band* members to her that she was going to be working with.

She was going to be singing *Mr. B's Blues;* a new song that Mr. Burbank had just composed and had written the lyrics too. Due to the tour commitments, the wedding was going to be a very small affair with only her immediate family in attendance.

Albert had sent a few photos of the wedding and a short letter, in which he wrote "*If loveliness were music,* then my wife would be a symphony."

After the tour was finished, they were going *via Vento* to her small home village for a couple of months and then they were going to settle in Rome as he had been offered a highly paid position, teaching music in an exclusive music school, *Vieni Su*, in the suburb of *Volare.*

I am positive that I would recognize Albert at the airport.

Now Frank was a different story; each time she had seen him, he had changed.

At one stage, he had gained a lot of weight and then he had lost it. He had grown a beard, and then shaved it off but he was always known as *the man with the golden arm* and hand. Whatever he set his mind to do, he did it and what ever goal he set for himself, he reached it.

He used to tell her as he was growing up; *I don't care if the sun don't shine; come rain or come shine, I'll never smile again* until I get what I want and when I want it. I'll work hard and save and I won't let much get in my way.

Well, he is smiling because he did get everything he wanted, even with a few setbacks occasionally.

I'm glad that he's getting in an hour before John because I don't know what John looks like. Frank would be able to be there to greet his own son.

The hardest person for me to recognize, would be Rose, or as dad would call her, *Rambling Rose*. I remember her as a long haired, fairly plumpish girl of *five foot two, eyes of blue*. She always said "I have *the gypsy in my soul"* and she was true about that. She was never a *goody, goody* child; in fact, she was the opposite and gave both our parents a hard time.

I remember one year, mom had a few words to say to her and she replied with "What do you mean when you say that I do all *these foolish things. What kind of fool* do you think I am, to think that just drinking *black coffee* will help me lose weight? I do eat plenty of food but I don't eat meat or fish, that's all."

I remember that we used to get a lot of postcards, letters and photos from her when she was travelling. I remember in one batch of photos she sent us, she had written on the back of them and one in particular had "*Me and my shadow* under the *blue skies* of *April in Paris.*"

Some months later, we received a postcard saying that she had a new friend named *Dolores* and they were heading *south of the boarder* to *Brazil.*

I know that mom and dad used to worry about her continuously travelling and often wondered how she got the money to pay for it.

Their answer came a few days after that when we received a rather long letter from Rose and in part of it she mentioned that spending *April in Paris* was fun and she had earned enough money from selling Honeycomb Bars and *Candy Kisses* at the *Happy Feet* Fun Parlor during the day and being *the peanut vendor in the cool, cool, cool of the evening,* to be able to move on. She was going to Rome *via Vento* and was hoping to catch up with Albert there.

The next thing we found out from Rose was that she was *south of the border* and she intended to stay there because she had just married Sam.

Together they bought and built up their travel agency "*Moments Like This*" and Sam; being a native of the country, took their clients on guided tours of well known places.

Nancy's thoughts were interrupted by her son, Shannon asking "Mom, dad wants to know if you have any more blankets for the caravan. *So far,* each bed has three blankets but as the caravan's outside away from the central heating, he would like to put more out there just in case Louise or John get cold *in the cool, cool, cool* of the early hours of the morning."

Nancy went to her linen closet and handed her son the two sleeping bags from the top shelf and said "*All I have to give you* are these sleeping bags.

Tell your father to unzip them fully and leave them folded at the bottom of their beds. John and Louise should be warm enough with the blankets and the sleeping bags.

When he's finished out there, *there are things* in here that I could use a hand in doing; like finish trimming the tree and putting up more decorations. Both you and Dean can help with the decorations."

A few minutes later, Dean came rushing through the back door panting and tried to say "Shannon told Michael that you were going to put up more decorations soon, so *I ran all the way home* to help you."

After their evening meal, Bob, Shannon and Lorraine went into the other room to start setting out more decorations to be put up and as Dean was helping his mother with the cleaning up he said "Mom, Michael was telling me that his auntie and uncle live down under in Australia and it is getting pretty hot during the days under *blue skies*. Don't they have Christmas down there?"

"Yes, Dean they do." answered his mother, "it's *Christmas time all over the world.*"

"But it can't be *Christmas time all over the world* if it's hot down there. I always thought that everyone had a *white Christmas* like we do." replied Dean.

His mother wiped her hands and then sat at the table and sat him on her knee and said "Some places in the world don't have snow because it never gets cold enough. In Australia, when it's winter, some places get a little bit of snow that is enough for the people to go skiing on. When it's time to do that, some Australians say *let it snow, let it snow, let it snow* so that we can go skiing.

No matter where you are in the world, most people at Christmas time will decorate a tree with *silver bells, mistletoe and holly,* sing a *Christmas song* and Christmas carols like *Silent Night* and *Jingle Bells* and other people will go to church to hear the choir sing carols like *O Little Town Of Bethlehem* and *Hark The Herald Angels Sing.*

There are even some people in the world who don't celebrate Christmas like we do because it's not what they believe in; but that shouldn't stop you from saying to people you meet "*Have yourself a merry little Christmas.*"

We are lucky in some ways, because we have a *winter wonderland* at Christmas but think of those people who don't have the snow and the cold; they think that they are the lucky ones because they can go to the beach and swim at Christmas time under *blue skies*.

Wouldn't you like to say *oh, what a beautiful morning* to be outside on the beach or would you rather hear me saying *Baby, it's cold outside* so put on your big jacket because it snowed heavily last night."

Dean sat quietly thinking and then turned to his mother and said "*Let it snow, let it snow, let it snow* because I like my Christmases with snow. I like it when we sit around the fire and sing *Silent Night, Jingle Bells* and *the Christmas song* that grandma taught us.

Mom, Michael also said that some people see and talk to angels. *How do you speak to an angel?"*

Now; it was Nancy's turn to think for a moment, and then she said "I'm not sure really. I think that you could speak to them after you say your prayers at night or you could just speak to them. Darling, I have never thought about it because sometimes I just ask for their help."

"Do they ever answer you?" asked Dean.

"Yes they do; but they don't talk to me like we are talking to each other. If I have an issue, sometimes they let me see something in a magazine that helps me solve it or if I have lost something, they help me find it while I'm doing something else. It may not be straight away or the next day but they do give me answers.

Now; how about we go and finish decorating the tree and you can put the angel on top. Wouldn't it be nice for everyone to see it sitting there when they get here?" replied his mother.

Dean went running to his father saying

"Dad, mom just said that I can put the angel on top of the tree. Can you lift me up please?"

The family spent the next couple of hours decorating the tree with extra *silver bells, mistletoe and holly* and singing *Jingle Bells* and *Silent Night*.

Sweet Lorraine was the first to go to bed, followed by the boys a half hour later. Nancy and Bob sat down, relaxed and watched their favorite *comedy* movie "*On An Evening In Roma Sault Ste Marie.*"

As usual, Bob fell asleep in the middle of the movie and when Nancy woke him, he again said to her "*Please don't tell me how the story ends* because once you do, I won't be able to fall asleep during it again 'cos I'll have to watch the entire movie to see if you are right."

Nancy said to Bob, "Before I turn in for the night, *I'm gonna sit right down and write myself a letter* well, not exactly a letter, but a check list of all the things that has to be done before mom and dad get here.

I will also have to write myself reminder notes for other things that have to be done and the shopping that's needed before Christmas Eve."

Jokingly, Bob replied *whispering* in her ear "When you're finished with them, give them to me because *I'm gonna paper all my walls with your love letters*. Maybe they will also remind me to do something one day.

Some days it may also stop me from *looking for yesterday* when I'm snowed under at work and thinking that *I'll never smile again* until I've finished off what Jack or Cindy was unable to complete."

Bob went off to bed and Nancy found her paper and pen and sat down at the kitchen table. As she was writing her lists, she recalled the questions that Dean had asked her earlier that evening.

The first question about Christmas was easy to answer but the second; how do you speak to an angel wasn't. Had she given him the right answer to satisfy his curiosity? She had never really spoken to or asked the angels for their help;

although there had been a few times that she had asked the Lord for his help.

She knew that most children had a good *imagination* at times and would often *make believe* that they were somewhere else in *far away places* or someone else whilst they were playing, but she never dreamed that of all people, Dean would ask such a question so seriously.

Bob walked into the kitchen for a glass of water and startled Nancy.

"*I'm sorry dear.* I didn't mean to startle you. Is everything alright because *the way you look tonight* and more so now makes me think that you seemed to be in a very deep thought." said Bob.

Nancy explained the conversation she had had with Dean and about the questions he had asked her. She told Bob what she had told Dean as a reply to his questions; however, she still felt unsure as to whether it was enough.

What she didn't tell Bob was that she had just seen and heard a nice looking man with amazing blue eyes and a cheeky smile looking and speaking to her through the kitchen window. He had disappeared as Bob walked into the room.

Bob said "If it wasn't enough, then he will ask more questions until he is satisfied. Why don't you try to bring up the subject with Rose and Sam; they might be able to give you some more answers.

I have heard stories that in the mountains of the Machu Piccu or was it the Sacred Valley that people have seen some sort of flying saucers and have seen strange people. It could also be some of *that old black magic* that people talk about. *Take me* for instance; I don't know if I believe in them or not."

He took his wife's hand and helped her up from the chair and then he pulled her close to him and continued saying "*Everybody loves somebody* and at this present moment, *I can't give you anything but love* so *let me love you tonight.*

A long time ago *you might have*

belonged to another but *you belong to me* now; besides *you are my sunshine* and you light up my life. You know that *I've got a crush on you* still and *you do something to me when you're smiling* that cheeky little smile of yours."

Before he could say anymore, Nancy gave him a *kiss* and gently pushed him away saying "*Let me go lover* or we will never get to bed. It *takes two to tango,* and for me *taking a chance on love* with you was the best thing I ever did." and as she was climbing the stairs to their room she whispered "*How d'ya like your eggs in the morning.*"

They both started to laugh but tried to keep it down so that they wouldn't wake the children.

IN LONDON AND PARIS

Frank and his family had been in England for nearly six weeks now and were all getting restless to go home. John, their eldest son, had met up with some of his friends from the Upper *Santa Lucia* University that he attended in Canada and had gone to Paris with them on the proviso that he caught the plane from Paris instead of travelling back to England to join his family for their trip to Chicago.

On the second day of their fifth week in England, Frank met with two of his hotel managers, Grazie and his wife, *Laura* and Prego, his wife *Dolores* and their daughter Irene, who was about the same age as his daughter Louise. Scusi and his wife June, and their son Adeste were held up and would be joining the rest of the group the following morning. Prego insisted that the group should dine together at the *Azure* Restaurant and then he would take them on a guided tour of *London by night.*

Irene asked her parents for permission to take Louise to the *Swing Low Sweet Chariot* Club one evening because they were *wingin' with rhythm and blues.*

She looked over to Louise and said "I think that you would love it there. It really is our place for the *birth of the blues* music. Not only do they play the blues but they do a dance called the Beguine. When you have finished dancing our style of the Beguine, you'll feel like you've been *dancing on the ceiling;* we *be-bop the Beguine."*

Prego replied to his daughter "It is alright with your mother and me; however, permission from Louise's parents should be sort before you make any plans. Don't forget, Adeste will be here tomorrow and it would not be nice to not include him. Taking him with you might give you some protection from some unscrupulous young men.

When I was younger, I heard of a few things that happened to young women who were on their own as I was *walkin' my baby back home."*

The following day started as *a foggy day in London town;* however, most of the fog had lifted by *about a quarter to nine* when the others met Scusi, his wife June and their son Adeste.

Adeste took one look at Louise and holding out his hand to her, he said "*Adeste Fideles* Rovelli. It is a pleasure to meet you."

Scusi looked at his son's delighted face and thought "You don't have *a ghost of a chance* with her, but then again; when I met your mother, *June in January,* just after the New Year's celebrations, I said to myself that *I don't stand a ghost of a chance with you* but after some time and a lot of perseverance I married her."

Grazie, Prego, Scusi and Frank left the women to work out what they were going to do for the rest of the day, while the men went off to begin their business meeting.

Dolores said "*What I've got in mind* for this morning is that we take Julie and Louise to the shopping district so they know where to go if they need to get some Christmas shopping. Laura or June, do you have any ideas on what we can do this afternoon?"

June replied "Not far from the shopping district are the street markets. They sell a multitude of goods including just about anything for the *body and soul*.

One of the best things about those markets is, they open at *daybreak* and remain open all day till *come sundown,* for that's when they close for the night. *Come rain or shine* or *a foggy day,* they will still be open.

My friend *Cecilia* runs the *Witchcraft* Coffee Shop there and she has incorporated a bookshop and a *body and soul* fragrance shop, into the café. The name of the coffee shop is quite unusual, but it does seem to bring the customers in by droves.

Are those plans alright with you Julie? I also think that for today, Louise, Irene and Adeste should stay with us even though Adeste may get a little bored."

The females had a wonderful day shopping and looking at all the different items for sale at the markets. Julie and Louise even got some ideas for Christmas presents for the family, especially for Rose; *body and soul* products that would be easy to pack, legal to take through customs and transport back to the States.

At times, Adeste grew a little bored, but every time he looked at Louise's face he thought "*I think I like you* and I really don't mind being the only male in this group and *I'll string along with you* because *when you're smiling* I feel lucky just being *close to you*.

I think that *I've got you under my skin* and I know that *I've got a crush on you* already. *I'm a fool to want you* because I have just met you so I'll have to be careful that I don't come on too strong, too quickly. I don't want to make the same mistake as I did when I was *once in love with Amy,* but I blew it big time and that left me with *no love, no nothing* but *oh lonesome me*.

I wonder if Louise and Irene will spend *tomorrow with me.* I could take them to the *Trade Winds* Gallery and Lookout.

On a clear day, when *that lucky old sun* is out visitors go up there to see the city of London and the surrounding districts.

I still like going up there because London is *my kind of town.* If *the lady loves to dance,* she will be able to pick up some really good music to *rock-a-bye your baby* with; that is if she has a boyfriend at home, from the gallery. I think that I'll ask them when we next stop for coffee."

The meeting between the men seemed to go reasonably well; however, Frank felt that Grazie still had something on his mind that he didn't want to mention during the meeting, so he was going to bring it up the next time they were on their own.

Over the meal that evening, Adeste was finally able to ask the girls to spend the following day with him; of course with their parent's permission.

He told them what his plans for the three of them were.

Laura said "Up at the Lookout if *that lucky old sun* is out, *on a clear day you can see forever,* especially if the wind is blowing the *smoke, smoke, smoke* away from the industrial district. If you know where to look, you can see the large house that *ol' MacDonald* built last century. *The folks who live on the hill* would like to pull it down because it is too old looking for their ritzy suburb, but the Historical Society won't let them do that because it has been certified under the Heritage listing.

Louise, you may be able to buy some musical gifts of our bands and singers for your relatives and friends back in the United States for Christmas.

There is a band called *Please Be Kind* and I think that they must have been recording since the *birth of the blue* first came here because *Sam's song* is *s'wonderful.* They are my favorite band at the moment.

If you know of someone who likes to read true stories; then try and get a copy of the book "*The Fable Of The Rose*" because the story is about when the MacDonald's first built and moved into their place and of *that old black magic* that was brought upon his family by *the naughty lady of Shady Lane.*

She used to dabble in *that old black magic* until she was arrested for being a witch. Mr. MacDonald could have saved her from being sent to the colonies, but he would not testify in her defence.

In one section, Charles MacDonald has been reported saying "One night when I was *walking my baby back home,* I told her that *I've got you under my skin* and I suddenly broke out in this very itchy but painful rash.

The female who I was with screamed out, "*Let me go lover* because I don't want to catch it from you." and ran home to her place.

I never saw her again and I was not able to go out in public until it had gone many years later."

"Oooh." said Louise before Laura could say any more "that sounds like a really good book. *Please don't tell me how the story ends* as I will buy the book and read it myself. Mom, I think that granddad would also like to read it. If I can get a copy for him for Christmas; I will.

I might even get a copy of the *Please Be Kind* music as I like listening to the blues every now and then. I wonder if *Sam's song* is anything like and as good as the *Cradle song* sung by the band *Goody, Goody."*

Laura laughed a little before saying "Some of the bands that are playing around the world these days have some very unusual names like *Goody, Goody, Please Be Kind, King Of The Road, Baby O* and *Auld Lang Syne.*

I wonder if the last band took their name from the song that we usually sing at midnight on New Year's Eve.

You young people of today; *you make me feel so young* with your music and dancing."

Adeste said "One of the best songs that I have is *Bee Bom One For My Baby* which is sung by *Goody, Goody.* The worst song out at the moment is

How It Lies, How It Lies, How It Lies and sung by your favorite band *Please Be Kind.*

Louise looked Adeste and said "It doesn't matter what type of music that you like or don't like; *it all depends on you.* Bands and singers are the same now as what they were in the past except for the difference in styles of music and lyrics. Some bands even revamp old songs and bring them out on their new albums.

Everyone has their own opinion and for most people *you can't love 'em all.* My dad loves all types of music except he just can't listen to Heavy Metal or Rap music and mom is not so bad. As I grew up playing with my dolls; mom used say that you have to *rock-a-bye your baby* to sleep so that a lot of noise won't wake them easily."

Because each family was staying in nearby hotels, they all agreed to meet at *about a quarter to nine* the following day at the Coffee Shop in Frank's Hotel, when they would each make their plans.

Frank asked Prego and Scusi to join them about half past nine; that would give him plenty of time to talk to Grazie about his issue.

That evening when they arrived back at their hotel, a bellboy informed them that they were to go to the front desk immediately.

When they reach the front desk, the hotel manager took them to his office and told them that just two hours before they had returned, the hotel had received a phone call from France from their son John. Unfortunately the message for them was never received as the phone call was cut off suddenly.

About half an hour later, the hotel staff was informed again by phone, to tell all their patrons that were to leave that evening for France, not to do so and then the line went dead again.

We are still trying to find out what is happening over there but contact with France; especially Paris, is very difficult at the moment. At present, there hasn't been any mention of anything in the overseas news broadcasts on the television or radio. The hotel manager told them that if the hotel receives anymore news about the incident, they would contact them immediately.

The manager also told them not to worry too much, as this incident has happened before when there was very heavy snow storms or really bad *stormy weather* in Europe and France.

The following morning, there was still no further news from France so Frank left a contact number with the hotel manager and Julie said that she would keep in contact with her husband during the day.

Louise met and went off with Irene and Adeste for the day. Laura, Dolores, June and Julie decided to go to the Matinee session of the new play "*Wham! Bam! Thank You Ma'am.*"

During the play Julie thought "That is supposed to be a *comedy* but *it's funny to everyone but me*. Maybe I don't see the funny side of it because I'm worried too much about John."

When they walked out side of the *Stardust* Theatre, Dolores said "*There's no business like show business,* now is there. I laughed all the way through."

June turned to Julie and said "Didn't you find that funny at all? I looked at you a couple of times and it seemed as if you wanted to be somewhere else instead of being here. I hope that there is nothing wrong between you and Frank?"

Julie apologized for her being so distant and explained about John and the night before and how worried she was. Then she said "*S'posin'* he was injured and needed me, *what can I do* when I don't know where he is. *Who can I turn to,* to find out?"

June said hesitantly "Haven't you heard. Yesterday afternoon *stormy weather* hit many surrounding suburbs of Paris and then it was followed by a very unusually large blizzard that affected nearly all of France.

The storm cut some of the power and telephone connections in Paris, but the blizzard cut roads, power and nearly all the communication networks.

It has also affected the airlines and railways. I think the tunnel under the river maybe the only way in or out of France. In really bad weather even *the river's too wide* to cross safely in boats or ferries."

Dolores looked up to see Irene running towards her shouting "Mum, mum, we've just heard about what has happened in France. We were *standing on the corner* by the lookout after we had just come down, when the paper boy started selling the early edition of the news. Isn't it terrible that the blizzard could cause such a landslide that has buried many houses in Lower Paris?

Rescuers are digging people out from *under the bridges of Paris* while other men are frantically trying to clear another *six bridges to cross* to the nearest towns to help rescue the villagers and tourists trapped there. Louise told us that her brother was in France with some of his university friends but she didn't know exactly where they would be."

Dolores turned and said to Julie "What university does John attend in Canada?"

"The Upper Santa Lucia University. Why?" replied Julie.

"Mum, doesn't Cousin Pierre attend the *Reaumur* Solitaire University near the Arc de Triomphe and isn't that the sister university of the one that John goes too?" asked Irene.

"Yes he does and yes it is." replied Dolores "and it is this time of the year when they hold many activities at that university and other universities in other towns?

If he and his friends are there, then they are safe because the university is on the north side of Paris, well away from the landslides.

Time after time we have had to go through this; waiting for news. The train line will be cleared in a couple of days and some of the phone lines will be repaired quite soon but *till then* all you can do is wait. I will try to contact my sister when I get home because her phone lines are usually repaired first as they are on the same grid that supplies the overseas lines."

Meanwhile Frank and Grazie sat down and talked about what was bothering Grazie.

Grazie said "It's just a problem that Laura and I have to work out. I think that she's *homesick that's all*. It happens the same time each year. Laura comes from a very large, close knit family who get together at Christmas.

We met while she was studying fashion design in Paris and we used to meet nearly every evening *under the bridges of Paris*. One Christmas, we travelled back to her home town of *Sault Ste Marie* high in the mountain near the Austrian/ Switzerland border.

The town was so high up in the mountains that I thought that we were going to travel *over the rainbow* and right *out of this world* just to get there.

That Christmas, I proposed to her and we made the arrangements for us to get married the following Christmas.

Just before we got married, I was

offered a placement in your hotel in London and to start work at the end of the following January and I accepted it.

We both knew that it would take a lot of hard work to set ourselves up; to find a place to live, for Laura to finish her last year at college and get work here in London and to save so that we could start a family.

We don't know why, but Laura doesn't seem to be able to give me any children. We have both seen many doctors and have had many tests but no answers can be given to us as to why she can't conceive.

We never talk much anymore and when we do, we usually end up fighting. She usually comes out with things like "*I'm always chasing rainbows* and *don't let the stars get in your eyes* while your chasing those *dreamy blues.*" or she'll say to me "*How it lies, how it lies, how it lies.*

You're a *dreamer with a penny* and you *won't be satisfied until you break my heart. Here I'll stay* with the *full moon and empty arms.*"

During the last fight she said "*Don't let the stars get in your way* while you search for your *impossible dream*. I don't think that *you belong to me* anymore. *If I loved you* anymore it would only because of the money you earn and give me."

I know that she doesn't mean it and I know that each year she writes to her parents telling them that *I'll be home for Christmas* but we never get there. This year I think that she has made plans to go home for Christmas and if I let her go alone; I know that it would be *bye, bye baby* and she wouldn't come back.

What kind of fool would I be, if I thought differently?

If we go together, then she will still want to stay there and for me to stay with her. I will have to give up my position in the hotel that I have worked so hard to gain. I just don't know what to do."

Frank and Grazie had just finished their conversation when Prego and Scusi walked into the room. From then on their business meeting involved menu changes for the different seasons, redecorating or renovating different sections of the hotels, devising new activities or sight seeing tours and the amount of new staff each hotel would need, plus a new budget to cover all the costs involved.

They even had ideas that they would try to implement for each different hotel if they were the managers there.

Three hours later Frank received a phone call from Julie telling him that they would all be there shortly as she has some news about France. As he hung up the phone from Julie's call, the hotel manager from where he was staying rang to say that there had been a little bit of news from France but he wasn't fully certain about the authenticity of the news.

Scusi looked at Frank and said "You look tired. Are you alright?"

Frank replied "*I couldn't sleep a wink last night* worrying over John and the France situation. I would like to go and look for him but I have no idea where to start looking.

The rail lines would be blocked and the airports would either be closed or on restricted flight landings. Even *Rudolph the red nosed reindeer* would have trouble landing there today.

The only other ways would be by sea or the tunnel. I know that when there is very bad *stormy weather, the river's too wide* for a safe sea crossing; so that only leaves the tunnel and I think that they would restrict entry into France at this point of time.

Julie and the girls are on their way over, so maybe *I'll know* more when they get here. *So far* we know very little and we are concerned for the safety of our son who is somewhere in Paris or another part of France."

"*Time after time* the people of France have to go through these disasters during the *stormy weather* of the winter months.

As time goes by, living in France, you learn to live with the *stormy weather* and you help out *where or when* you can, when you are needed.

The citizens of France will rally around

and help each other and by *April in Paris* you will never know that this disaster has happened.

Don't be afraid for the safety of your son because I'm sure that he is in a safe place with people who will look after him." replied Grazie reassuringly.

Julie was the first through the door of the meeting room with the other ladies and the young people close behind.

Julie hurried up to Frank and said pantingly "Dolores's sister rang with the news that John was with Pierre, her son and a few other lads and that they were safe. Evidently *the boys' night out* last *Saturday night* had ended in Rouen; a fair distance away from Paris where most of the trouble was. John also passed on the message that *somehow* Pierre will get me back to London via the tunnel and *I'll be seeing you* next *Saturday night* at your hotel."

"Dolores, please thank your sister for relaying that wonderful news to us. *You'll never know* just how much it means to all of us.

Now, *what I've got in mind* is that we all go out for drinks to celebrate the good news before *two sleepy people,* or maybe more, get an early night.

As we have nearly finished our business here, may I suggest that tomorrow can be a day off for everyone; so please enjoy yourselves and rest and relax.

I have heard that over at the *Stardust* Theatre there is a new play called *Wham! Bam! Thank you ma'am*. I have also heard that it is supposed to be funny and I think that I could do with a bit of laughter at the moment. We will meet back here on Friday morning at ten o'clock. Now, who's for that drink?" said Frank.

The next two days passed very quickly and John arrived back in London on the Friday, instead of the Saturday, on a *Parody Medley* Adventure coach. *Mam'selle Medley,* a friend of Pierre's, arranged with her father to transport John back to his parents for their flight back to Canada.

When John was reunited with his family

he told them about his little adventure. He told them that if they had stayed at the University for *five minutes more,* it would have been *too close for comfort* because reports of what had happened two miles down the road from the University had not been mentioned.

"You know how *I've had feelings before* something was going to happen; well I had that feeling again while we were in the *Birth Of The Blues* Club.

I yelled out "*Johnny get your girl* and you *guys & dolls* come with me now. I'll tell you why later, but come on it's *time to go,* NOW."

We went to *Medley Monologue's* place and had just arrived there when the *stormy weather* hit and the power went out. As we drove up the drive, Medley said "This is *the house I live in* with my father and he won't let me see my mother because he claims that *the lady is a tramp* and since the divorce she has become *the naughty lady of Shady Lane.*"

She didn't *mention a mansion* as the house she lived in.

It looked *too marvelous for words.* She said that her father spent a lot of time doing business in the many towns along the *road to Mandalay,* or *on a little street in Singapore* or *on a slow boat to China.*

One day, when she lived with her mother, her father came home from a business trip and found her in her mother's place of business and became angry and shouted "*What's a kid like you doing in a place like this?*" and took her back to his house to live there permanently.

Medley seems to be a *lonely girl* and if I went to the University in Paris, *we could have been the closest of friends.* I know that we can still be friends and write to each other, but our studies will have to come first.

My personal property that is in Paris has been sent to the airport for me to collect before we leave on Sunday.

Mr. *Monologue* has taken care of the flight arrangements and has me on the same flight to *Chicago* as you, mom and Louise."

Early the following morning, the airline that Frank and his family were to fly with on the Sunday, rang to ask them if it was possible for them to travel together that day, Saturday instead.

They explained that due to what had happened in France that week, the airline had to rearrange their schedule to include extra flights. If they were to fly on the Sunday, they would most probably have to fly separately instead of together. Their flight would be leaving in three hours if they wanted to fly together.

Waiting at the airport for John to arrive was *Medley Monologue*. As she spotted John, she walked up to him and startled him by saying "*Hey there,* I think that you would need this if you intend leaving England." and she handed him his bum bag that contained his wallet, passport and other official papers.

Then she said "you left the bag under your coat as we left the *Birth Of The Blues* Club. I put it in my bag so that it did not get lost and was meaning to give it back to you but it was very hectic at the time.

I was watching you from across the table, because *I only have eyes for you,* and you looked like you were looking and listening to someone just before you made us leave. Am I right?

You know that I was just about to say to Pierre "*Hey brother, pour the wine* or you can *drink to me only with thine eyes* but I prefer the liquid stuff better. That is just a little joke between Pierre and me.

He was *once in love with Amy* and she ditched him for some other guy. I know, I was *young and foolish* and *fools rush in* to situations without thinking first. Well I ran, because *I've never been in love before* and I thought that I could stop Pierre from getting *a blues serenade;* but he told me that we could only be *just friends* as he saw me more as a little sister.

That night was when the little joke started. I am comfortable with our friendship; in fact, I'm glad it didn't become *too romantic."*

I gave my father your bag so that he

could change all your travel arrangements and you were lucky I did because all flights are booked out for the next two months. Many people have to travel to Italy, Germany or Spain to connect with their flights.

There has been major damage done at the airport, so no flights will be able to land or take off until all the repairs are completed. It might even take a week before any sort of flights to be able to land.

I will say goodbye to you now, but please remember *memories are made of this* and I will miss *the sunshine of your smile*. When we first moved over here, *I left my heart in San Francisco* but now, Paris is *my kind of town* and you are welcome to come and share it with us anytime you like. Goodbye."

IN ITALY

"What do you mean; *we open in Venice* for a six week run next week? You know Vincent; that my wife, family and I leave for our two week holiday in three days' time. This holiday has been arranged for over six months now and Francesca is supposed to be taking all my work for me while I'm away. Why are you not talking to Francesca instead of me?" asked Albert in a very loud voice.

"We cannot find Francesca anywhere. He has not been home for three days now and his mother does not know where he is. We have even been to the *Mambo Italiano* Club where he usually meets with the *guys and dolls* and they said that they last saw him going into the *Solitaire Bar* last *Saturday night.*" replied Vincent.

Wait here a moment. "*Oh Marie,* have you seen or heard from Francesca in the past two days. He seems to have gone missing and we need to find him immediately." enquired Albert.

"The last time I spoke to Francesca, he said that he was going to take *Amor* out *on an evening in Roma*.
He was picking her up at *that Old Black Magic* Music Hall in *Memory Lane* after her performance of *My Funny Valentine* had closed for the evening." said Marie, Francesca's receptionist.

"*That's Amore Reprise,* right. I don't know why he is going out with her; *the lady is a tramp* and will have him *makin' Whoopee* wine and *standing on the corner* selling it *in the blue of the evening just for fun.*

I think that I had better go and see if I can locate him and talk to him. I need to get him back here so that I can have my holiday.

Oh Marie. Would you please ask Mr. *Volare Sway* to come and see me in the morning? If I can't find Francesca then I'll see if *Volare* can step in for the time I will be gone. Thank you." replied Albert.

At home that evening, Albert decided to discuss the disappearance of Francesca with his wife Marie and then their children; for it would concern them all. He called his children to the kitchen where his wife already had been informed of the situation.

"*You'd better sit down kids*. I have something to discuss with you." said Albert and proceeded to tell them a part of what was going on at work.

Romeo, his eldest son asked "Papa, if you can't find Francesca and Mr. *Sway* can't stand in for you; does that mean that you won't be able to *come fly with me* and the rest of us back to the States to be with your family over Christmas?"

A loud disappointed sigh came from the other children and then his daughter Christina said "Well, if you can't go then *here I'll stay,* with you. How can you *have yourself a merry little Christmas* on your own? You kept writing to Aunt Nancy telling her "*I'll be home for Christmas"* and you were looking forward to seeing your family again, and now you're saying that you can't go with us.

Every time we say goodbye to you as you travel to *far away places* with your work *I'd cry like a baby* when I go to bed, *that's how much I love you*. I am not *glad to be unhappy* but I know that *we'll be together again* soon. Katrina told me the other day that *you're nobody 'till somebody loves* you but I know that you are somebody and we all love you."

Then she turned to her brother Antonio and asked "*How about you* Tony, will you stay here with us?"

"*What'll I do,* I don't know yet. Papa has not yet said if he is not able to go.

He said that he is going to ask Mr. *Sway* if he can step in. *I believe* that he will step in and we will all be going on holidays together." replied Antonio.

"Alright now children." said their mama "*everybody loves somebody* and you are all *easy to love* that's why we all love each other.

Now, how about loving me some more because it's time to get ready for bed; without the arguments please.

Don't forget to *kiss* your papa goodnight Christina. Romeo, give your teeth a longer brushing tonight and

Antonio, put your dirty clothes in the wash basket and not on your floor before you climb into bed. We will be up shortly."

Marie looked at her husband and said softly "*Aren't you glad you're you.* Christina really is *exactly like you.* I think that she would give her *heart and soul* to make you happy this Christmas if you have to stay here. I would not feel right leaving you behind neither; however, all the arrangements have been made and the tickets are all paid for.

Nancy would have gone to a lot of trouble to get her place in order so that she could accommodate and feed us all."

"*Oh Marie, you are my sunshine* and *you are my lucky star.* When I first met you, *you brought a new kind of love to me* and I am so happy that *you belong to me.*

I still remember *me 'n' you 'n' the moon* when we were out *on an evening in Roma,* especially *when you're smiling* like you are now. *You and your beautiful eyes* are all I need to remind me that

I will always have *one foot in heaven* when I'm with you. *If I loved you* any more than I do now; my heart would burst through my chest."

As he stood behind her and put his arms around her waist, he whispered in her ear "*You do something to me* and now I want to get *close to you*. I will do everything I can to be with you and my family for Christmas. I will even cancel the engagement if I have to, *that's how much I love you* and the children."

Marie un-wrapped the hands that were holding her and said "*Let me go lover,* the children are waiting for us upstairs. Our *love & marriage* will always remain strong just as long as we work on it *day by day*. We all have to make sacrifices along the way but the sacrifice that you are willing to make now; shows me that *I got the sun in the morning* and *it's a lovely day tomorrow*.

Now don't let *fools rush in* too quickly. Wait and see what *Volare* says first, and then we can discuss it further before you start cancelling your engagements.

Now; let's go and say goodnight to the children and then we'll discuss *what I've got in mind* in our room."

"Why, Mrs. Dawson, has that *old devil moon* been shining in your eyes again? Just to think, that I have *all this and heaven too;* it's *too marvelous for words."* whispered Albert in his wife's ear.

The following morning, Vincent arrived at the office just as Albert arrived. Vincent appeared to look angry and when questioned, he said "I saw Francesca with *the naughty lady of Shady Lane* and I approached him to ask when he was coming back to work.

He told me that "*I've gotta be me* and *love is the tender trap* that I have never been caught up in before. People say that *the lady is a tramp* but *oh! Look at me now; my heart has found a new home now* and *there's no business like show business* especially when *money burns a hole in my pocket.*

I now work at *That Old Black Magic* Club singing *Sam's song* and the *money song* which is the *closing tune.*

Oh! Lonesome me has now gone and *I've got my love to keep me warm* each night."

He also said that I was jealous of him because *I ain't got nobody* in my life here in Italy because I left *April in Paris."*

I replied to his remarks by saying "*Don't let the stars get in your eyes* and you don't know *what is this thing called love* is anyway. *You came a long way from St Louis* to play in the orchestra and now *that's Amore* has gone to your head and you have a *devil may care* attitude. *It's only a paper moon* that you see each night and where there's *smoke, smoke, smoke,* there's fire and trouble.

Some enchanted evening when you *take your girlie to the movies,* she will excuse herself for a minute and that's when you will find out how it feels *when your lover has gone* for good. That's when *the birth of the blues* will start and you will try to find ways to pull yourself together.

One night when you go out for a meal, you will find out the truth; *the lady is a tramp*. After a few drinks you may approach her and ask "*Is you is or is you ain't my baby?*"

She will *make believe* that she doesn't know you and say that *you might have belonged to another* but not to her. She will make you feel like the *Chattanoogie shoe shine boy* lost in *autumn in New York.*"

Francesca laughed at me then said "*I don't care if the sun don't shine* in *April in Paris* or in *autumn in New York; everybody loves somebody* and *as long as she needs me,* I will stay with her. Tell Albert that I'm sorry but I won't be back."

And then he walked away down *Memory Lane* towards *That Old Black Magic* Club.

Vincent said "It took *all of me* and my strength to keep from losing my temper at him and..."

The men were interrupted when Angela, Albert's receptionist, knocked on the door announcing the arrival of Mr. *Volare Sway.*

"*Volare.*" said Albert as he entered the

office. "How are you? I have a proposition to put to you and it could be to your advantage."

Albert explained to *Volare* the recent happening with Francesca and then asked him if he would be interested in the upcoming engagement in Venice.

Albert also told *Volare* that if he was interested; Francesca's job was going to have to be filled as soon as possible and considering he knew what the work entailed, if he would like to take it on; then he would certainly be welcome.

After the engagement in Venice, there were several other engagements to be fulfilled in a few cities that were on the *road to Mandalay* and the music company was also involved in negotiations to take the troupe of actors of a new theatre play called "*Mighty Lak' A Rose*" on a slow boat to China cruise for a month.

Volare responded by saying "I thought that I saw Francesca coming out of *Memory Lane* a couple of nights ago.

I was *walkin my baby back home* after we had gone out for a few drinks at the

Amor Milk Bar just around the corner.

My little Peg is home on holidays and she has grown so much. She stays with her grandparents whilst she is in school, now that her mother is no longer with us. It doesn't matter how much she grows, she will always be the *Peg o my heart.*

Peg actually leaves later this afternoon to go back to her grandparents and my contract with *Ring – A – Ding – Ding* finished last week; so yes I can substitute for you in Venice and *yes indeed* I would like to replace Francesca in this company. *Ring – A – Ding – Ding* was only casual work, so I think that a full time permanent job would be really nice for a change. I could still see my Peg during the school holidays because she would be able to come to where I am playing.

Thank you for considering me for both positions."

Albert was very quiet when he arrived home and after the family had finished their meal he said in a softer tone "I'm sorry, but I'm afraid... that we will all be going on holidays together this year.

Volare is not only going to substitute for me in Venice but he has also agreed to join the company. With him in the company, it will mean that I will not be going away as much. I will still have to go away; but not as often. I will be doing much more work in the office."

Christina shouted "*Oh boy! Oh boy! Oh boy! Oh boy! Oh boy!* When I said my prayers last night I asked the Lord to *please be kind* to our family this Christmas.

The funny thing was, when I put my *head on my pillow,* I heard a man's voice telling me to practice *the Christmas song* and *the Christmas waltz* because I will have to show Uncle Sam how to do it.

The voice also said that Cousin Louise is going to teach us how to *be-pop the Beguine.*

I was not scared and I did ask the voice to *come out wherever you are* but I must have just gone straight to sleep."

Romeo the eldest of the boys said shyly "*I have dreamed* during the last two nights that I was asked by *someone like you* papa to "*Come fly with me* and he would *fly me to the moon* and back. He said that he wanted me to see *my blue heaven* but I wasn't going to die.

He also told me that *I've got the world on a string* because *love is all that matters* and *what could be more beautiful* than the love of the family.

He also said that when we come back, we will *come back to Sorrento* and we will find many *pennies from heaven* there. Papa, have you any idea who the man is or what he means, or was it just my *imagination* playing tricks on me while I was asleep."

Antonio said "When we *come back to Sorrento*. We're not going back there, we're coming home, aren't we papa?"

As Albert went to answer his son, he saw a strange look come across his son's face and became concerned and asked "Son, son are you alright? What is happening? Do you feel ill? Do you want us to call the doctor?"

"Huh! Oh, no papa, I'm alright." said Antonio a few seconds later. "It's just that I saw a man with blue eyes and long hair, the same color as Christina's, standing by the back door and I heard him say that on Christmas Day you have to *get me to the church on time,* because *none but the lonely heart without a song* will know what Christmas and love is all about.

He also said that *you're nobody till somebody loves* you and that *you're gonna love yourself in the morning when you're smiling. I've got you under my skin* and you'll stay there for many more years to come."

Antonio turned to his mother and said "He told me to tell you this "You toss *three coins in the fountain* and *we kiss in a shadow. You are love* and *my shining hour* but *my lady loves to dance* to the *melody of love. My heart stood still* as *my funny valentine* walked down *on the sunny side of the street.*"

Papa spoke to me and the man just disappeared.

Mama are you alright, you have gone white in the face."

Albert looked at his wife and said "All those years ago. Do you think it could be...?"

Marie shook her head and whispered "I don't know. Let me think about it. I might mention it to Rose when I see her and see what she thinks." then raising her voice a little louder she continued saying "Today we will finalize the packing and you children can help me finish wrapping the gifts. *I'm gonna sit right down and write myself a letter* for the things that need to be done."

"Mama." said Christina "don't you mean that you are going to write a list; not a letter."

IN PERU

"*Stella by starlight,* that's a beautiful picture. I think that *I'm gonna paper my walls with your love letters* and drawings, starting with this one. Do you want to help me? Now where shall we start?" said Rose.

"Stella, Stella, oh! There you are? *Hey won't you play* games with me now? I have been waiting for you to come out into the back garden. *I get a kick out of you* when you want to play *fly me to the moon* on your swing." said Nasha.

Stella replied "*Here comes the night* and papa and Inka will be home soon with the wood to make *smoke, smoke, smoke* and fire to warm our house for the night.

When *I got the sun in the morning* in my room tomorrow, then I come and play with you, alright. We can also help mama to plant the *sunflower* seeds in the garden, now that the birdies have sung their *September song* and I have said *bye, bye blackbird,* have a good holiday."

As she walked through the back door Inka said "*Hey there,* Nasha. Are you still playing with Stella?

Papa and me are *gonna build a mountain* out of wood and mud and *we're gonna roll* and stack logs to the edge of *Olman river.*

Mrs. Denue prays that the *river stay away from my door* and yours each time we have big rains. She is also hoping that we get *blue skies* on the day that we leave on our holidays."

Nasha said "When do you leave again? And how long will you be gone for?

I still remember the preparations that our families and villagers were making for Christmas last year but not for this year. You know I can still remember *the things we did last summer* school break. Do you remember that book you were reading that I wanted to read?"

"Yes, *Out Of This World.*" replied Inka "I remember because you said *please don't tell me how the story ends.* Did you ever read that book?"

"Not yet. I'm a slow reader and I'm still

reading *The Lady Is A Tramp*.

Papa took Zen and me over to watch *the birth of the Blues* new puppies. Mr. Blues told papa to pick one out and we can have it once it is old enough to leave its mama.

Zen wants to call it *That's Amore* but I want to call it *Dreamer*.

I know papa and mama will choose a suitable name for it." replied Nasha and then asked "Do you still want *peace on earth* this year for Christmas? You want that every year."

Sadly Inka said "Yes I do because *what the world needs now is love* and lots of it.

If people would only love their neighbours, then that love would spread down the street, across each neighbourhood, across each town, city, country and then the world.

Everybody loves somebody or so they should but there are too many greedy and nasty people who only love money and can only sing *the Money song* and that makes it seem bad for everyone.

If I loved you and *you belong to me*

and my family and we were happy, wouldn't you feel as if you're special and wouldn't you want to make someone else feel like that?"

Nasha thought for a moment and then said "Yes. *What the world needs now is love;* you're right about that, but they also need to give love as well as take it.

People also need to have faith in God as he will eventually make the world right.

We know that we are not the only ones on this earth and we know and believe in angels, but many people don't believe in those sorts of things. They think that the only things that come from *out of this world* are in the movies.

Uncle Tim was telling us about that when he came to visit us after his big business trip that took him half way around the world. What are you doing tomorrow?"

"Not sure, *how about you?"* asked Inka.

"Dunno, I'm gonna wait to see if *I got the sun in the morning.* I'm goin' home now. I'll see you tomorrow." said Nasha.

"Mama." said Inka "Nasha just told me that many people don't believe in angels. Is that true? Do you believe in angels?"

"Yes Inka, it is true but some people won't *say it* or even tell you if they do because they believe and feel that *these foolish things* only belong in the minds of little children.

Take me; when I was your age, I used to talk to the angel friend that I used to play with sometimes. *As time goes by,* you grow older and other things take your mind over and you forget about the playmate of your childhood.

It was during my travels before I met your papa that I began seeing and hearing from the angels again.

I was just about to say *goodnight Irene* at her front gate when we saw *a fella with an umbrella* walking down the street.

I never thought of it again until a few years later when I was in France, in the *2020* Club. I heard this voice say *hey there* and turned to see who I thought was Irene, who I hadn't seen for years.

Irene was not there but the fella with an umbrella was standing there handing me some chips and quite adamantly suggested in a whispering voice "*hey won't you play* your favorite number for the next five games."

I did and I won enough money to leave France and visit my brother in Rome, before I went back home to my parents place.

I was going to Rome *via Vento* when that *old devil moon* decided to upset my travel plans. *Accidents will happen* at any time; however, I don't believe in accidents. *I believe* that everything happens for a reason.

My friend Delores left me stranded when she met some other friends of hers who were in *Sammy's March* for freedom.

I knew that *every time we say goodbye,* she would always end up in trouble but I still decided not to go on *Sammy's March* with her.

A few days later, I heard that someone called the *sweetheart of Signa Chi* had the group arrested and deported.

That night the fella with the umbrella came to me from out of nowhere while I was walking home.

He told me "*You'll never walk alone* because *I'm walking behind you* and *all of me* and my kind will always watch over *all of you* and your family.

You have never believed that *you're nobody until somebody loves you* because *when you're smiling,* you bring love and joy to everyone around you.

When you see *the lamplighters serenade* sign and you hear *the coffee song, you're gonna love yourself* and someone special who will provide you *the good life* the way that you want to live it."

The *Saturday night* before I was to leave Rome, I was sitting at an outside table in a café when I heard "And *it came upon a midnight clear* that I come to you *as you desire me. At long last love* has walked into my life."

I turned to see your papa walking up to me and I replied "That is such a stupid thing to say to get someone's attention."

He laughed and said "I could have said now *ain't that a kick in the head* or *drink to me with only thine eyes* or *how d'ya like your eggs in the morning* or my favorite *Bop! Goes my heart.* Which one do you like best? Mind if I sit down?

Oh, I had better introduce myself first so that I won't be a complete stranger to you. I'm Sam and you are?"

I looked into his eyes and I had to agree that Bop! Goes my heart was the best because that was what my heart actually did do.

He sat opposite me and I felt comfortable with him. The waitress came out to get his order and he said "Coffee for me and *one for my baby* as well."

He then asked me what I was going to be doing that evening because *Saturday night is the loneliest night* of the week if you are all alone and suggested, if I wanted to, that I could go with him *on an evening with Roma, Swannee* and Carrie to the Lamplighters Serenade outdoor picture show just down the street, *just for fun* and company.

Afterwards they were going to the *Mambo Italiano* Arena to *be-bop the Beguine* and go into a specially constructed room that was made from mirrors where it would look like you were *dancing on the ceiling.*"

I looked at him and said "*Never before* has anyone come up to me and been so quick to ask me out like you have. *I'll string along with you* for a while because *memories are made of this* and other *once in a lifetime* encounters."

I told your papa that I had told my sister *not so long ago* that I had a gypsy soul and that my papa used to call me rambling Rose and that I was leaving Rome in a few days but I wasn't sure of where I was actually heading for. I didn't know if I was going home or down to South America for a look around.

He told me that he was going home in a few days as well and he lived in Peru and would I like to travel with him."

Sam walked through the door and said "That's right and your mama and I came to South America and *it happened* in *Monterey* on *some enchanted evening* beneath that *old devil moon* that I realized that I was in love with your mama.

I was *once in love with Amy,* a girl I met France; well, I thought I was until I met your mama. *Our love affair* grew and she stopped me from being a *dreamer.*

After we got married, we still travelled around South America and that's when your mama and I bought the travel agency and you came along, my little *Inka Tinka* and then a few years later, our little *Stella by starlight.*

Now let's get some of your things ready for our holiday."

Once the girls were settled in bed for the night Sam and Rose talked about Sam's next guided tour which was only going to be a two day trip to Cusco and then the other tour guide would take over and finish the tour so Sam could get back to leave for his long awaited holiday to Chicago.

Rose asked "Has Inka ever asked you about angels and if you believe in them?"

"No." replied Sam "why; has she asked you?"

"That's what we started talking about when you came in. Nasha told Inka that her uncle Tim told Nasha that many people don't believe in angels and Inka didn't understand why. I think that's because we live in such an unusual place, Inka has grown up and takes for granted that everyone believes in UFOs and angels.

I hope that my family doesn't think that she's making things up if she starts talking about them and that we have encouraged her to believe it." Rose said quietly.

Sam's reply was "I don't think that they will take any notice of her; in fact, they maybe fascinated by what she tells them.

Other people might just think that she has a vivid *imagination* or that she is a *beautiful dreamer;* however, we are only going to be there for a couple of weeks and then we'll be home again so it won't matter what the other people think.

Some think *I'm crazy to love you,* but I

don't care about them; all I know is that *if you were the only girl in the world,* I would still love you forever and a day. After all these years *I only have eyes for you* and *I've got you under my skin* still and you lodged yourself there with our first *kiss*.

That afternoon I knew that *my heart has found a new home now* and I always want it to stay there. I always want to be *close to you,* so come here you *embraceable you* and *kiss me again* so that I can find out if *I've got you under my skin*.

Yep, *my heart tells me* that you are still there."

The girls were up early and Sam left for his tour to Cusco.

Nasha rushed in and excitedly said to Inka "Papa was telling mama when he came back from feeding the animals that he saw another disc from *out of this world* heading in the direction of the Machu Picchu Mountains.

He said that he wasn't sure of *where or when* but *that old black magic* will soon be felt in the air and it will mean that it will be *the tender trip* and the *last call for love* for some people."

"*Hey there* and good morning to you Nasha." said Inka "*Jeepers Creepers,* why do you get so excited when you hear about the discs. You should know that *everybody loves somebody* but sometimes they need a little help to get it in motion.

Sometimes, just a few *moments in the moonlight* or a walk under the *blue skies* just *east of the sun* or just sitting with a special someone at the café; listening to the *Coffee Song* can have people *bewitched. Until you love someone* you will never know what will happen and you are too young to love someone in that way and so am I."

"Inka, why do you always end up sounding so grown up." replied Nasha "*What kind of fool am I* to think that we are ready to fall in love at our age?"

Stella interrupted Nasha by saying "*Hey won't you play* with me outside on the swing Nasha? We can play *fly me to the moon* because mama says that I have to have *someone to watch over me* in case I fall down and hurt myself.

I got the sun in the morning through my window so I knew that I can play outside today but really; *I don't care if the sun don't shine* as long as it is not raining, then I can play."

"*Hey there Stella by starlight,* yes, I'll come out and play with you for a little while. Are you coming too Inka?" said Nasha.

Inka replied "You two go and I'll be out in a moment. I want to talk to mama first."

As the two girls went outside, Inka found her mother in the kitchen just finishing cleaning up after their breakfast and asked "Mama, *why was I born* so grown up?"

"What do you mean?" asked her mama inquisitively.

"Nasha says that I talk like a grown up and I'm not." replied Inka.

"Darling." said her mama "you think and talk differently than Nasha and sometimes that makes you sound like a grown up.

Don't forget that you are in a higher grade at school than what Nasha is and at home here you read a lot and ask questions that your papa and I answer as honestly as we can.

You always want to learn more than some other children. It is not a bad thing to want to learn and you will then be able to answer questions that Stella may ask you in the future.

Now run along and go play with the others for a while because this afternoon I will need your help to make sure that everything we need for our holiday is packed because your papa won't be here to help me."

"Mama, *I'm glad there is you* to answer my questions. *Who can I turn to* for answers if *there's no you* here for me?

Papa goes away for work a lot and the neighbours think that I'm too young to understand some stuff.

I love you mama and *if I could write a book* about the things that you and papa have taught me, I would. You know one day I might just do that." replied Inka seriously as she walked over to her mama to give her a hug and a *kiss*.

What Inka had just said to her mama, surprised Rose and as she made herself a cup of coffee, she began to think. "*I could write a book* too. I could write about my younger years growing up at home with my brothers and sister, the things that mom and dad taught me that enabled me to travel.

All my travelling experiences and the sort of work that I had to do to get the *pennies from heaven* to continue my travels until I met Sam in Rome and my life changed for the better.

Now; *what did I have that I don't have now?* I had a lot then, but I have more now and *as long as I live* I will never regret getting married to Sam and having my two wonderful girls.

I know at times they can be a handful and *all of me* wishes that I was single again but *fools rush in* when you are tired and stressed and *that old feeling* can creep back in to your mind.

I only have to look at Sam or either of the girls and I realize that *nothing could be finer* than what my life is right at that moment. Without them I would be *oh lonesome me* and drifting from place to place trying to find out where I belong.

I still remember that man who spoke to me many years ago and that he said "*You'll never walk alone.*" and he was right.

He also said that my family would never walk alone either but I wonder what he meant by that?

"Mama! Mama!" shouted Stella and Inka, as they came racing through the back door.

"Mama, a man with an umbrella just told us to tell you that what you are thinking was right and you will learn what he meant when we are on holidays.

He also told me that I would be like you and would learn more than anyone can but I would always be safe and that I would always have *someone to watch over me.*

He told Stella that she would be a star in years to come and would help many people. You and papa will be very proud of her.

He turned to Nasha and told her to tell her mama that Huahuqui and Chasqui are here and she would understand it and explain it to everyone.

I didn't see him until he spoke to me and I didn't see him go and all I remember of him is his nice smile and his blue eyes because he was standing in front of a big white light.

Who is he mama and how did he know we lived here? Could he be one of those people from *out of this world?*" shouted Inka.

"Yes, he was a really nice man but I no see him too?" said Stella as she came running in after her sister.

"Slow down and *speak low* so that I can hear you properly. Now you just told me that a man spoke to you, but you couldn't see him properly because of a big white light behind him. Is that right?" asked their mama.

"Yes" said Inka "should we go and see Nasha's mama because the man said he was back and that she knows all about it?"

"Not yet. We should wait and see if they come over here to see us and tell us what is going on. I wish your papa was here because he might know who the man is." replied their mama.

It was a few hours later that Nasha and her mama visited Rose and the girls and tried to explain what had happened that morning.

Rose already knew how to speak Spanish; which was the main language in Peru but once she had married Sam, Rose had learned to speak Quechua, so that she could communicate with the other villagers.

She was able to understand what Nasha's mama had said; yet still she wasn't quite sure of what it meant. It was an interesting conversation with Nasha's mama and even though Rose knew that she and the girls were safe; she still wished that Sam was there with them.

That night Rose had the best night sleep that she had ever had when Sam was away. Normally when *it came upon a midnight clear,* Rose would still be awake.

The following day passed very quickly and it was *in the blue of the evening* when Sam finally walked through the door to the welcome of his family.

The girls went off to bed as did Rose and Sam because they had to get up very early to get to the airport for their flight to Chicago.

It was on the plane that Rose told Sam about the events of the man that spoke to the children and of Nasha's mama's explanation and asked him if he knew what it meant. Sam nodded but said nothing for a while.

He looked out the window and seemed to be deep in thought. Rose was hoping that Sam would tell her something about what she had told him before they touched down in Chicago, which was only an hour away.

While Sam was still looking out the rain

splashed window deep in thought; Stella started asking all sorts of questions, mainly about Christmas and her other relatives that she has never seen or met.

Then she asked "Mama, *Where do you keep your heart* so no-one can steal it?

I just heard the man over there tell the lady sitting beside him that she should lock her heart away and *put your dreams away* with it."

Rose replied "*When you're smiling, you are too beautiful* to be able to lock your heart away. Your smile comes from the love in your heart and sometimes it shows through your eyes as well. Never lock your heart away. You're just a child that is learning all about life and you have so many wonderful experiences to look forward to and go through.

One day when you have grown up and have children of your own you will never have to ask "*Which way did my heart go?*" because it will always be where it is now."

Sam turned from the window and said to Stella "When I was a little boy living near the Machu Picchu Mountains, *a little bird told me* that *I'll never smile again* if I locked my heart away and that I should always be a *dreamer* because *without a song* and a *dream* in my heart I'll never share *some enchanted evening* with someone special.

At the moment you are like the *sunflower* seed that is just pushing through the earth and in a few more years you will be fully grown into a beautiful flower."

Their conversation was broken by the announcement that they will be landing in Chicago in a few minutes. The excitement of seeing all of their relatives seemed to make the girls more talkative than ever.

Sam never did explain to Rose what Nasha's mum had meant about the message that was given to her, so Rose intended to ask Sam later that evening.

THE ARRIVALS

Nancy was up early, long before the rest of her family was. She had so much on her mind that she said to herself out loud "*I'm gonna sit right down and write myself a letter* to remind me of all the things that I have to do today and also add a space for things that I have to remember for later on today or tomorrow."

Bob walked through the kitchen door and said "*Hey there, embraceable you.* I think that instead of writing a letter, you should write yourself a couple of lists and put them on the fridge or the notice board and then you can mark off the jobs once you have done them, but you can also add to the other one; things that you remember that you have to do as you go along.

Now sit down and start writing while I make us some coffee. I'll see to the children's breakfasts this morning and the cleaning up and you just concentrate on the things that need to be done before we have to start the trips to the airport to pick everyone up.

I think that seeing all your family again will be *s'wonderful.* In a way I'm glad that they are not all arriving on the same day as it would be so hectic here."

Bob was interrupted when Shannon called out "Mom, Uncle Frank is on the phone and he's calling from London."

Nancy raced to the phone thinking that something was wrong and a few minutes later returned to the kitchen and said "Frank and all his family will be arriving this afternoon at two o'clock. He said that the airline had to change their flight to today and he would explain it when he gets here.

He only had a few minutes to let us know of the changes because his flight was boarding."

The phone rang again and Nancy went to answer it. She came back into the kitchen, looked at Bob and said "It's going to be hectic here today and we are going to need both cars to go to the airport.

Rose and her family are boarding their flight in an hour and she said that *I'll be seeing you* in a couple of hours.

I thought that she wrote that her family was leaving tomorrow?"

"I don't know how we are going to work this out. We will have to do shuttle trips between flights but I can't just bring my family home and then leave them alone here while I do another airport run." said Nancy.

"Mom." said Shannon, who had gone into the kitchen, "we can pick up nanna and granddad and you can bring them home here and I'll come back with you. I am big enough to be left with them and help them settle in and make them a cup tea. I'm sure that they will be no trouble for me to look after."

Bob and Nancy laughed and then Bob said "That is a good idea Shannon. You are old enough to help out and I'm sure that your grandparents won't give you any trouble.

Thank you for offering and thinking of the idea.

Now I think that it's nearly time to start leaving for the airport. Lorraine, you had better get your big jacket because *baby it's cold outside*.

Who wants to come with me?"

"Just *five minutes more.*" said Nancy. "I'll go to the Domestic Terminal and wait for mom and dad and you head for the International Terminal for whoever arrives there first. I think that it will be Rose and her family. I think that Frank and Albert are arriving this afternoon."

Bob went over and put his arms around Nancy and said "Everything will be alright and will run smoothly today and *do you know why?* Because you are very organized and are very calm during a crisis or when plans have to be changes suddenly.

Just think; *memories are made of this* and other things that will be happening over the next few weeks."

Nancy gave Bob a kiss on the cheek and whispered in his ear "Thank you for those reassuring word and you're right, *memories are made of this* and next year we will be thinking back and laughing over this, but now you have to *let me go lover* or we will be late and I don't want my parents worrying about us because we are not there to meet them.

Please don't talk about me when I'm gone to the others about how I am so nervous and excited in seeing them again."

"Don't worry; I won't say anything to anyone. So let's go and meet them and *smile darn ya smile. When you're smiling;* you seem to *powder your face with sunshine* and no one knows what you're going through inside." replied Bob.

At the Domestic Terminal, Nancy met her parents and on the way home she explained to them what was happening that day with the rest of the family and that Shannon was going to stay with them whilst she went back to the airport.

Shannon said "Mom, *while you are gone,* may I show granddad and nanna the new renovations that have been done so they will know the changes before everyone else gets here."

"Yes Shannon; that would be a good idea. Could you please make sure that the caravan is unlocked so that Louise and John can put their luggage out there when they arrive?

Some people down the street think that you are *young and foolish* and they may be right at times, but today you are being very thoughtful and acting in a grown up manner and I thank you for that." replied his mother.

Back at the International Terminal, Nancy found Bob standing by the counter with the other children.

"The plane from Peru has been delayed due to *stormy weather* and will be arriving just before Frank and Albert and their families are due to touch down.

Both of their flights are running ahead of schedule. I think I may have been wrong when I said today could be hectic; I think it's going to be worse than that.

The trouble is; will we have enough room in both cars for all us to go home together?" questioned Bob.

Nancy replied "I have the bigger vehicle

so we may have to squeeze them into my car and try to fit the luggage in your car. Otherwise, you can take the first arrivals home with the children and leave them there with Shannon and my parents and I will wait for the others to arrive and for you to come back.

You know it may take a while for them to get through customs especially if there are multiple planes landing from overseas. When we can find out more, I'll give Shannon a call and tell him what's going on."

"*If I loved you* any more than I do now, it would only be because I have found something extra to *all the things you are* now and you are *too marvelous for words* as it is.

You are *my funny Valentine* and I will *always* love you *night and day*. When I said that *I can't give you anything but love;* you took it, but in return you have given me not only love but a very practical thinking, loving and supportive woman who can solve issues quite quickly." Bob said.

The three planes touched down in Chicago one after another and taxied to three different terminals away from each other.

That meant that her two brothers had arrived at different ends of the terminal and her sister had arrived in the middle of the terminal.

Nancy turned to Bob and said "You said that I was very organized and very calm during a crisis or when plans have to be changes suddenly, but how can I work this one out? I don't know how to be in two places at the same time? Have you any suggestions?"

Bob thought for a moment then replied "First we'll see who has arrived at what terminal and then I'll go to the one that is the farthest away. You can then meet the other one and then we can meet at the middle.

Rose and her family will most probably get through customs first because they are not really coming from overseas.

We can ask them to wait so we can greet your brothers and then we can work out how we are going to get them all home."

Dean pulled on his mother's arm and said "When Aunty Rose gets out here, *here I'll stay* with her so she won't be on her own.

I know that I am not as old as Shannon but I can still help out.

I don't think that someone will try to take me if I stay with Aunty Rose and her family because other people will think that I am with them.

Mom, *what I've got in mind* is; couldn't we hire one of those buses that carry a lot of people for a couple of hours.

That way we can take everyone home and some of the luggage in it and dad can put the rest of the luggage in your car and follow us home. Dad can bring the bus back and then come home in his car."

Bob looked at Dean and then at Nancy and said "Dean has just come up with a logical solution and *I don't know why* I didn't think of that.

I don't think that you could *call me*

irresponsible or you either, if we left him with Rose and her family for a few minutes while we go and get the others.

I'll go over to the desk and enquire about hiring a bus if there is one available? *How about you?* What do you think of Dean's idea?"

Nancy looked at Bob and replied "What are you still standing here for? This is not going to be one of those *same old Saturday nights* tonight."

Bob was only gone for a few minutes and when he returned he was holding some keys in his hand. "I have to have the bus back in three hours." he said.

Bob hurried down to the far end terminal because that was where Frank, Julie, John and Louise were coming through customs and where they had to collect their luggage from.

Bob had just left when Rose, Sam and the two girls walked out of their terminal with their luggage in tow.

Nancy greeted them, told them the scenario and left Dean with them while she and Lorraine hurried off in the other direction to meet Albert, Marie and their three children.

Albert and his family were delayed for a few minutes in customs due to another passenger from their flight not declaring some items they were bringing in to the country. It didn't take long for custom officers to sort out delay.

It took about ten minutes for Bob and Nancy with the help of John and Albert to load Nancy's car with most of the luggage, and the families and the remaining luggage in the bus. Even though there was a lot of traffic leaving the airport, everyone was back at Nancy and Bob's house in just under an hour.

Shannon had given his grandparents a tour of their house so once the rest of the families arrived; they could help unload the vehicles. Bob set off with Dean to take the bus back and within the hour they were pulling up back into their driveway.

Before they went inside the house Bob said to Dean "*Day by day,* I see you grow and change and *because of you* and your quick thinking today, you saved your mother and me a lot of running around.

Thank you and I'm very proud of you for acting so grown up. Now go inside and enjoy being with your cousins."

Bob could hear some excited little girls running around shaking *silver bells* and shouting *Santa Claus is coming to town* and *Rudolf the Red Nosed Reindeer* is bringing him."

As Bob walked through the door he heard Frank yell out to Albert "*Hey brother pour the wine,* Bob's back and I think that he could do with a drink."

Albert replied "He'll need more than one wine to get him through. With all of us here I think that even a barrel of wine won't be enough for him."

That comment started every one laughing.

Christina, Inka and Louise went into the lounge room to look at the Christmas tree. Romeo, Shannon, Dean and Antonio went up into the boy's bedroom to play some games. Lorraine and Stella sat playing with dolls near their mothers who were talking with all the other women.

Each were discussing menus, children's eating times and bedtimes so that they could work out a quick and simple plan that allowed each of them the chance to rest and relax each evening.

Rose commented "When I said that you didn't *mention a mansion* that you lived in, I was right. This is a mansion especially from where I come from.

Up in the Machu Picchu Mountains nearly a whole village would live in a place like this and they would think that they are kings and queens."

Nancy said "Now does anyone need to do any shopping before Christmas Day?

If we need to buy food supplies, then we women can go and get it and leave the children here with their fathers but if presents for someone are required then I suggest that we catch the tram into the city. We could walk but the *river's too wide* for the younger children to walk on a cold day.

On a clear day, you could walk to the

city *on the sunny side of the street."*

Sylvia said that she and Fred still had to buy some gifts and Julie also said that they had a few more to get.

So after talking with their respective husbands, everyone would get up early and a trip into the city would be made by tram. The children seemed to like the idea as well, so they were packed off to bed early.

Louise and John decided to go to bed as well, leaving the grown-ups to sit and catch up on what has been going on in their lives since they last saw each other.

Sylvia looked at Marie and said *"Oh Marie,* I hope that you are not feeling awkward with us being together. We had never met you before you married Albert and this family get together might be a shock for you. I know that you may come from a large family yourself but you are here in amongst strangers in a different country."

Albert took his wife's hand and said *"I am loved and this is my beloved* Marie who has stuck by me and encouraged me to get us where we are today.

We often talk about our families to each other and to the children. I even told them the story of when Frank and I went *swinging down the lane* to the beach where we thought we saw *shadows on the sand* that scared us.

We took off through the nearby park and over the rope bridge that crossed the *ol' man river* that began to *sway* with our combined weight.

Frank yelled at me to hurry because *something's gotta give* out and the rope might break.

Well, *somewhere along the way* over it did start to break and we got off it just before it did break. If we had been on that rope bridge for *just a moment more,* we could have been seriously injured when we fell into the river.

We swore that we would never let you or dad, know about it mom because we knew we would be in big trouble. Now *I don't care who knows* because it is one of *these foolish things* that you do when you're growing up."

"Yes, it was *too close for comfort* but do you remember the lady who was there and helped us and the unusual blonde haired man who as he walked past said "*Luck be a lady* and *anything goes* in life.

Life, yes, *she's funny that way* but she will always be good to you. It's just one of those things that you have to get through *night and day, nevertheless, pennies from heaven* will always fall your way." asked Frank.

John had just walked back inside and listened to the story and made the comment "*There is nothin' like a dame* to help you out when you're in trouble." and proceeded to tell them all about what had happened to him in France; how he got out to meet up with his parents in London and why their flight was changed.

Fred stated that he was tired after having a hectic day and was heading off to bed. Sylvia said the same and before long everyone was heading for their respective sleeping quarters.

Rose had intended to ask Sam about the message but was too tired to lie awake talking; besides they might have woken Stella, who then would have wanted to get up and play. She also knew that they had to get up early for their trip to the city.

It was surprising to Nancy that everyone was up so early even her own family because she normally would have to call each one of them several times before they made an appearance for breakfast.

Stella told Nancy that at home when *I got the sun in the morning* in my bedroom, it means that I have to get up. Sometimes *I don't care if the sun don't shine* because that means that *that lucky old sun* is staying in bed for the morning and has sent the rain clouds along to give the plants and animals a drink.

I think that the sun would *tell me at midnight* if he was going to stay in bed but I'm fast asleep by then.

The mothers were the only ones allowed in the kitchen once the men had their coffees and teas. Breakfasts were made and eaten, the dishes were done and the kitchen was tidied, and now to get everyone ready for the day out to the city.

Louise was the one who took the longest to get ready because she couldn't make up her mind what to wear and in the end, it was her grandfather who said "Louise; just *stay as you are*. You're going to town and most of the time you will have your big coat on while you're outside because it's so cold."

Stella saw the unhappy look on Louise's face and walked up to her and gave her a cuddle around her legs because she couldn't reach any higher.

As she was doing this, she looked up to Louise's face and said "When I am sad my mama tells me to go and *powder your face with sunshine* and *smile darn ya smile* like the angels do. When she says that to me; I know that *somebody loves me*, and I don't feel like "*oh lonesome me*" any more."

Louise picked up her cousin and gave her a big hug and replied to her "Yes Stella, *everybody loves somebody* and your mother will always love you and so will the rest of your family.

All of me is feeling a lot better now. I think that I am ready to go out now. *How about you?"*

Even though the walk to the tram stop was not very far, the younger children enjoyed running around in the very light ground covering of snow that had fallen over night.

Fred whispered in Sylvia's ear "This may be the last time that we are all together like this so take it all in my dear. I don't have to ask myself anymore, like I did when I was younger, *what did I have that I don't have now* because *I've got the world on a string* now and it's *because your mine,* our children and our grandchildren.

I couldn't ask for anything more to make me so happy because that's *how much I love you* and them."

Sylvia quietly replied "Yes my dear, *memories are made of this* and *the nearness of you* will always be *my shining hour* whether it is *night or day* on a

Sunday, Monday or always. If we don't stop whispering to each other, *people will say we're in love."*

The last comment from Sylvia made them both laugh.

Chicago was a big bustling city to Sam and Rose's children and there were so many things that they had never seen before.

There was a very large and tall decorated Christmas tree standing in the city square and at its base stood a choir of people singing Christmas carols like *God Rest Ye Merry Gentlemen* and *Hark! The Herald Angels Sing.*

Not far from the tree, in front of the *Birth Of The Blues* Café, the *Chattanoogie Shoe Shine Boy* was whistling the *Christmas Waltz* whilst he was shining shoes for his customers.

There was a boy playing a trumpet outside the very crowded *Luck Be A Lady* Bar and Grill on the opposite side of the tree.

The boy sounded like he was just *learnin' the blues* because he kept stopping; however, he played a lot better *the second time around.*

When it was time to find a place to eat, everyone seemed to want something different so the family decided to go to the *That's Amore* Bongo Room Eatery where all their taste buds could be met.

Sam and Rose had the Vegetarian Wraps and the girls had Waffles and Ice-cream.

Nancy and Bob had toasted sandwiches, the boys had a pie each and Lorraine had fries.

Frank, Julie, John and Louise also had toasted sandwiches. Albert and Marie each had a Chicken Wrap instead of a pasta meal, while the boys order burgers with ketchup.

Christina whispered something in Romeo's ear and he called out to his father "Papa and *one for my baby* sister but without pickles please."

Fred and Sylvia decided on tea for two, a Bagel with cream cheese and slices of Apple Tea cake that they would share.

When they left the Eatery, each family decided to go their own way and meet back near the Christmas tree at about four o'clock.

The rest of the afternoon went flying by and everyone bought their last minute gifts and wrapping paper.

Louise asked John what he had bought for his friend Karen, from the Santa Lucia University and he replied "*My lady loves to dance* so I bought her the latest *Jeepers Creepers* Album. *Guess I'll Hang My Tears Out To Dry* is the new single off the album and *they say it's wonderful* and the best album that they have released. I'm sure that she will like it."

Louise ran into an old school friend, Angela who was with a male person. "*Hey there* Louise." shouted Angela "I thought that you were in England? What are you doing here in Chicago?

Just before school finished *was the last time I saw you;* wasn't it?

Oh, sorry. I am so rude; *this is my beloved* Tom and we have come here to visit his elderly aunt.

Actually Tom has been here for nearly three weeks now because his aunt has not been well.

She had said to him "*Who can I turn to* when I need someone in times of need."

I felt like *oh lonesome me* back home so I came down two days ago to spend Christmas with him.

We have just bought an *American Beauty Rose* for his aunt to plant in her garden next spring. It should be alright if we keep it inside in the pot until the weather gets warmer."

Tom said "I was *walking my baby back home* one *some enchanted evening* and told her that my aunt was not well and that I would have to come to spend Christmas here looking after her.

I rang her at the beginning of the week and asked her to *send me the pillow that you dream* on because I missed her so much and she has done one better; she has come here in person and *there's my lover* for you."

Tom looked at Angela and continued saying "*you're getting to be a habit with me* and a good one at that. I know it *takes two to tango* but if you and I talk out any issues that arise; then I'll know that *somebody loves me* in the right way and I will always have *someone to watch over me night and day*.

Yes baby, *you go to my head* and *you do something to me* that will never make me sing the *September song* and say *bye, bye baby. You belong to me* now and *what kind of fool* would I be if I let the love of my life, *my funny valentine* slip through my fingers."

Louise replied "This year for Christmas we are having a family reunion at my Aunt Nancy's place. We arrived back from England yesterday and will be spending the next two weeks here before we head back home.

Sorry, I've got to run. We'll have to catch up sometime when I get home."

John asked "She was once your best friend; wasn't she? What happened to change that?"

Louise quietly said "Yes she was; *we could have been the closest of friends* but now *the lady is a tramp*.

I know Tom as well. He asked me to go out with him several times but I said no. *Saturday night is the loneliest night of the week* but I prefer to spend it alone rather than spend it with him and his mates drinking.

You and I know that I don't drink and don't really enjoy just sitting around with people who do it to excess.

Don't tell me to *please be kind* and *try a little tenderness* with Angela because she will not listen to any advice when she asks for it. I know a few things that Angela has told me about her home life and *something's gotta give* with her soon. *Till then* she has to live her own life her way.

Now let's not talk about it anymore or you'll spoil my day."

On the tram going back home there were eight very tired but very excited young children because they knew it was Christmas Eve and that Santa was coming that night.

Their parents knew that it would be

easy for them to get their children into bed early and that would give them time to wrap the remaining presents and to sit and talk peacefully with the other adults.

Lorraine asked "Daddy, how can Santa visit all the people in just one night?"

Frank replied "It's *all in a nights work* for him and don't forget he has Rudolph and the other reindeers to help him.

It's just like me going to work during the day where I have other people to help me; well, Santa works *after hours* when it is quieter and there are no planes in the sky to get in his way."

Nancy said just before they got off the tram "Now *all of you* children will have to have quick showers tonight before your evening meal and then we can set up the plate for Santa and his reindeer before you go to bed.

Louise, will you be able to supervise the showering of the children and maybe bath Lorraine and Stella for me please?"

Just after they had got off the tram, a dog ran past them and Inka started to tell Romeo, Shannon, Dean and Antonio about the *birth of the Blues* puppies. She also told them that her friend Nasha would be getting one as soon as it was old enough to leave its mama.

Just before getting into bed, Antonio said "Papa do you remember when I saw that man with the blue eyes and long hair, the same color as Christina's, standing by the back door, and I heard him say that on Christmas Day you have to get me to the church on time, because none but the lonely heart without a song in their heart will know what Christmas and love is all about.

Well, do you think that there is a church nearby that we can go to in the morning or do you think that I should forget about it?"

Albert looked at his son surprisingly and replied "I am not sure yet. I will talk to Nancy and see if there is a church nearby and I will let you know tomorrow, first thing in the morning. Now you run on up to bed. Good night."

Julie picked up on the description of the man and asked Albert about it.

Nancy also questioned Albert about the same man who she had seen in the previous few days.

Nancy turned to Rose and asked her if she wouldn't mind coming out to the kitchen with her as there was something puzzling her and she wanted to discuss it with her.

She turned to the rest of her family and jokingly said "*Please don't talk about me when I'm gone*. I know that *just for you* I make a good humorous story."

Nancy and Rose were in the kitchen talking for about an hour when Bob and Sam came in to make some hot drinks for the others.

Nancy then told Bob that she had been talking about the questions that Dean had asked; especially the one about how do you talk to angels?"

Sam's face turned a little pale and said "After we have made the hot drinks, I think that we all should go back into the other room and I will explain something to all of you. It will also give you the answer to what Nasha's mother has said.

I have dreamed that I would have to sit and talk to all the family about this person; however I had hoped that the subject would not have come up."

THE FAMILY'S MEMORIES

As Nancy, Bob, Rose and Sam came back into the living room carrying the hot drinks, everyone went silent.

Sylvia said "We have just been discussing what Antonio said to Albert and it seems that at some time or another during our lives most of us here has had some sort of encounter with this or a similar male.

I don't understand what it means. Do you Rose or Sam?"

"I think I do." said Sam "but before I tell you my story. I would like to hear all your stories and your family's stories. As you are the parents, why don't you go first Sylvia and tell us if anyone has said or done anything to you?"

Sylvia said "Alright but it may be nothing at all and *please be kind* to this old lady because I am not going crazy. I hadn't long met your father when I went back to San Francisco for a holiday.

You see at the time I thought that *I left my heart in San Francisco* with my old boyfriend. We went to Las Vegas for a few days on business, so he told me, and whilst I was there I found out that he was *spoken for* and he was cheating on me.

I was standing by a slot machine when I suddenly saw the reflection of a very handsome man with a beautiful smile and sensuous blue eyes standing behind me, in one.

I tried to turn around but I was frozen on the spot and he said to me "*You'll never walk alone* and if you go back to the park, *you're gonna love yourself* even more on your return because there lies love and *memories are made of this* and many more beautiful things and happenings in life.

If you *powder your face with sunshine* every morning you will always be *young at heart*. Life is like a dance, you *begin the beguine* and before long you find out that it takes two to tango.

You will never live on the street of dreams because yours will always come true.

If you look east of the sun, west of the moon on a foggy day you will find *my shining hour.* On the sunny side of the street is where you will always live until the day after forever. Life is so unpredictable, yep, life, *she's funny that way.*

It was then that I came home and married your father. I must confess that I have had the most wonderful life that a person could have given me. You could never *call me irresponsible* for getting married at such a young age nor having you children when I did."

Fred looked at his wife and said "I have wanted to tell you this many times but I also had an encounter with this man and he told me that I will mention it when the right time comes and I think that time is now.

I remember he told me "*Something's gotta give* and in the cool, cool, cool of the evening something will give and that will change your life in a good way forever. If fools rush in to love and find that they have made a mistake, then this time you are no fool and you have not made a mistake.

Have a little sympathy and *try a little tenderness* in the beginning and your love will be colored with polka dots and moonbeams and *out of this world* with happiness.

Life is so unpredictable, yep, life, *she's funny that way,* but the saying that *you're nobody till somebody loves you* is not true because somebody will see something in you, that will attract you to them. It could be *when you're smiling,* so *smile darn ya smile,* or in your devil may care, happy-go-lucky attitude.

You will be lucky but will that *luck be a lady* that will make you feel like the king of the road or something else?

It's a lovely day tomorrow and that's when you will find out. Somewhere along the way you will mention me to others but until that time comes, and you will know when the time is, please don't talk about me when I'm gone."

When he asked if my luck would be a lady I can honestly say yes to that question. The best time of all was when I was *walking my baby back home* after a night out, with the *smoke, smoke, smoke* that was in the air from the wood fires of the nearby houses and not to *mention a mansion* or two, on the cold winter evenings before *we kiss in a shadow* of a big old oak tree.

After we were married I used to think about Sylvia's old boyfriend and I used to say to myself "*Who's sorry now.* Not me, but you would be if you knew the kind of woman that you gave up. I am so glad that your mother came back to *Monologue* and me."

"Actually, I have had two encounters with this so called man." said Frank "the first one was when I was a young man starting my first job.

He came to me in a dream and told me that I would become very successful and that when I married and had children, they would be very supportive of me and would want for nothing. He also said that my family would always be safe and protected.

The second encounter came when we were in London a few days ago as I went *through a long sleepless night* waiting for news about John.

A particular manager of one of my hotels was having issues at home with his wife.

The man told me that if I transferred this manager to the hotel in France, his home life would settle down, his wife would be happier and she would fall pregnant within a month of the transfer. The manager of the hotel in France could be transferred with the manager of the hotel in Spain and the manager in Spain could go to our second hotel in London.

He then reminded me that John was safe and protected and I would hear from him the next day. And we did."

Sam asked "Can you transfer these people around like he suggested?"

Frank replied "*Yes I can* and I think that it may have solved a few other issues that I have been trying to avoid.

I knew things weren't right over there and that *something's gotta give* and that's why we went over there.

I took the family with me so that they could have a holiday in a place that they had never been to before; except I didn't expect to spend time worrying about my son.

Because of the busy Christmas period, I have already informed the managers of the transfers and they all seem delighted with the moves that will take place in the first week of February.

Julie's father said to me once " *You take your girlie to the movies* and before long you are playing the *closing tune* on your single life. *If my friends could see me now* and *if I knew then what I know now;* they would not believe the way my life has turned out.

I told Julie once "I was *dedicated to you* and your mother and sang the *money song* everyday but unfortunately *money burns a hole in my pocket* and I got into a bit of strife. *What kind of fool am I* now? A big one!

If I had listened to your mother in the first place and learned to trust in myself and her and saved our money and not spent it foolishly then *our love affair* would have lasted longer than what it did. *Who's sorry now?* I am, and I only have myself to blame. Don't you ever make the same mistakes as I did?"

Julie finished the last of her coffee and said "I remember dad telling you that. He used to tell all the single males that if you *take your girlie to the movies* you would end up marrying them.

I remember having an invisible friend right up to the age of ten, that's when dad left for work one day and never, came home. Five years later he contacted my mother and asked if he could start visiting me again.

In my mind I could see and hear my friend and we used to talk for hours every day. She called herself my shadow as she was always with me.

She had the most beautiful smile and blue eyes and she also had such pretty soft blonde curly hair that hung down past her shoulders and she had such a great *personality.*

I used to say to her "*You are too beautiful* to be my shadow." On the first visit to my father, *me and my shadow* went to the park and we heard the birds singing the *September song* and my shadow said *bye, bye blackbird,* and all you other birds, enjoy your flight.

That day, after *me & my shadow* got home, she told me a few things including that I would meet a man who would be *easy to love*.

She also told me that the man I would marry would never say *love me or leave me* to me and I would never have to say *love me or leave me* to him.

You did *take your girl to the movies and then you kissed me* and from that moment on I knew that *you brought a new kind of love to me* that would last a life time.

I never used to like you going away on business trips because *everytime we say goodbye* I would always say to myself *lover come back to me because you're mine* and don't do what my father did to my mother.

Once you had returned from your business trip, you always became the *embraceable you* and you used to *hold me* so tight that I had trouble breathing.

My friend also told me that the rest of my life would always be happy and my children would always be safe. That was the last time I saw her or heard from her until John's "mishap" as she called it in London.

She told me to have faith and that he was safe and away from all the trouble. He would contact us and we would fly home together.

And yes, she was right about everything she had told me. In fact, I have had a lot more given to me than what she had told me."

Julie looked at Frank and continued "when I said that *I can't give you anything but love;* you accepted it, but after all these years that we have been married, *I've got you under my skin* still and *I only have eyes for you* and I always will have."

Sam asked if John or Louise have had

any sort of encounter of any kind.

Louise said "I had an invisible friend just like Julie had and Julie described her perfectly. We would just sit and talk and if there was something bothering me, then I would talk with her before talking to mom.

My friend didn't have a name that I can remember and she only stayed with me until I started my second year at school.

She did tell me things and said that I would remember them as I grew older. I do remember that she said that I would always be safe and protected and she would warn me if I was in danger.

My family would also be kept safe at all times.

Dad, she told me "When you meet the man that you will marry, he will be *someone like you. Till then, please be kind* to everyone who comes into your life.

When you're smiling you could *shake down the stars* from heaven. *Saturday night is the loneliest night of the week;* however you will never have a lonely

Saturday night because you will have many friends and so much love surrounding you." That's all I can remember at this moment."

John said "Over the years I have always had feelings if trouble was at hand.

In France, just before the storms hit, I had this feeling that my friends and I were in danger.

Only this time I heard a voice telling me to get out quick and head north. My friends and I were going to be alright and that I would be flying home with my parents. All the arrangements had been made.

I didn't understand what I had heard and I didn't have time to try and find out either. *What kind of fool am I* to stand around trying to figure things out when our lives were in danger?

I just knew that we had to get out the place and quickly.

Medley Monologue's father got me back to London in a tour bus and arranged all my changed travel arrangements.

Or, so I thought he had. Other than that I haven't seen or heard anyone before."

Albert interrupted the conversation by saying "I have never had any contact with anybody like that, but I do believe that angels do exist. I have had my troubles but I thought that it was my faith that brought me through them.

Oh Marie, I think that you should tell them about Antonio and the message that you received from him."

Marie looked down as if she didn't want to talk about it and said in a lower tone in her voice "In my religion, it is not customary to mention hearing or seeing angels or different beings and one day I let this story slip to Albert.

When I was growing up on a small vineyard in Italy; several times a year we would go to Rome to visit my uncle and papa would do some business.

One year when I was about sixteen we went to Rome and during that visit, my cousins and I visited the Trevi Fountain.

While we were there, a street cleaner snuck up on us and began talking to us.

He had an unusual accent but he looked the same as each description from the others here who have just told us their stories.

He told us that we should also visit the Sistine Chapel and the Vatican Museums. He told my cousin Regina that although we were all *young at heart;* a couple of us would sing the *September Song* later in life.

He also told her that *lonely is the name* of the game that she would play until she reached her mid-twenties and then she would *begin the beguine* and not the dance.

He told my cousin Visconti that he would play several instruments and would travel. Everywhere that he would go, he would get great applause and during an *encore* someone would yell out "*Hey won't you play* us your signature tune. You know; *One for My Baby.*"

He then turned to me and said "You toss three coins in the fountain and we kiss in a shadow. You are love and my shining hour but my lady loves to dance to the melody of love. My heart stood still as my funny valentine walked down on the sunny side of the street.

You have a beautiful voice and *the birth of the blues* has not started with you but you will carry it on. I cannot tell you *where or when* but you will meet your *lover* when you sing Mr. B's song and believe it or not; *the song is you*.

The *impressions* that you give will attract many friends but when you're out *on an evening with Roma* and *when you're smiling* is when your life will change for the better.

You will never be cold in any place that you go because you will say "*I've got love to keep me warm,* the love of my family and friends."

I will tell you one thing; he has been right with a few things that he has said. The other things have not come to pass yet.

I am not the only one in my family who has been visited by the same man. My three children have also had some encounter with him.

One morning, Romeo said to his papa "I have dreamed during the last two nights that I was asked by someone like you papa to go fly with him to the moon and back because he wanted to show him his blue heaven but I wasn't going to die.

He was also told that he had the world on a string and the love of his family was all that mattered.

We are not going back there, but he was told that there was money for us when we went back to Sorrento.

Romeo was confused and asked Albert if he knew what the man meant or was it his imagination playing tricks with him while he was asleep.

Now with Antonio; I think it may have been a day or two before we left that Antonio had his encounter with the man.

While Albert was talking with him, he went pale and we thought that he was getting sick.

He told us that he was alright but he had just seen a man with the same color hair as his sister and he told him that he should go to church on Christmas Day because something about lonely people will find out what love is all about whilst they are there.

He also told Antonio that *you're nobody till somebody loves you* and that *you're gonna love yourself in the morning when you're smiling.*

Evidently that's when the man gave Antonio the message that I just told you.

Now Christina went to bed as she always does and about the same time as the boy's encounter with the man, she had her encounter with him.

She said that she heard him telling her that she had to practice the Christmas song and the Christmas waltz because she will have to teach Sam how to do it.

He also told her that Louise will be teaching her how to be-bop the Beguine.

I have a feeling that he has told her more but she is not sharing that information with us at the moment and I don't want to push her for it.

Christina told us that she wasn't scared and asked the man to come out from where he was hiding but she said she must have gone off to sleep before he came out."

Nancy said "Sometimes I have heard Lorraine talking to herself while she is playing alone and once I went into her room to see if she was alright because she seemed to be getting upset with someone.

When I asked her what she was getting upset over, she told me that her friend was going away when she starts school and that she had said to her friend that *you won't be satisfied until you break my heart*.

I didn't realize that Lorraine knew such big words and that she was capable of stringing a sentence together like that; especially as she is so young.

Lorraine asked me to tell her friend that it was alright for her to stay as long as she wanted to. I asked Lorraine what her friend looked like and she held up one of her dolls.

She also said that her friend told her to *please be kind* and not to *rock-a-bye-*

your baby that way as she could end up hurting it.

The doll looks just like the person that you have all described and I'll show you all tomorrow. I took it that the doll was the friend she was talking to. Now after hearing what all you others has had to say; I'm not quite so sure.

Dean asked me the other day about "how do you talk to angels?"

One of his friends mentioned something to him and he came and asked me. I didn't really know what to say so I answered him the best way I could.

What kind of fool am I to think that I was able to give him an explanation that would cover his question completely?

That is what I was talking to Rose about in the kitchen this evening.

Shannon has never said or asked me anything that was out of the ordinary. Has he spoken to you at all Bob?"

Bob replied "No, Shannon hasn't spoken to me about anything except for the times when the UFOs are written about in the papers.

He asks me a few questions about them and if I believed that they were real. I told him that I wasn't sure and he left it at that.

As for this other person who seems to have visited everyone else and who has taken up most of this evening; I personally do not believe in angels, even though a couple of them are mentioned in the bible and I have certainly not had any contact with them.

I did have, what seemed like a very real dream one night when I was in boarding school in South Africa and *so far* nothing of that dream has happened or come true."

"Oh." said Nancy "you have never told me that you have had a dream. You always say that you don't dream. Are you going to tell us about your dream or don't you remember it?"

Bob replied "Of course I remember most of it but I don't think that it would interest any of you."

"You never know what may interest us." said Sam "so please tell us what you do remember."

Bob began "Well, it was a warm night in September, which was quite unusual for that time of year.

During the day I heard quite a lot of birds singing the *September song* and I knew that it would only be a few weeks more before I was going to go home for the holidays. My parents, who had been away on a cruise, were looking forward to spending time with me before we visited my grandparents in Delaware.

I dreamt that I was working as a dance instructor and when I told them that we would *begin the Beguine*, I would take them through it step by step.

One regular female student wanted me to partner her because, as she put it, *I dream of you* every night and *I only have eyes for you. I get a kick out of you* and the way you teach the dances.

The next minute all these *guys and dolls* walked over to me and said "*Let's get away from it all* and we can *begin the Beguine* down at the *Birth Of The Blues* Club down the road.

One of the guys told the female student "*I'll be seeing you* dance with Bob when I dance with *June in January* during the *Winter Wonderland* Ball, *O till then, please be kind* and leave him alone and before you say *we could have been the closest of friends,* let me remind you that you belong at home with your parents until you at least finish school."

As I turned to walk out the studio door, I found myself standing on a river bank looking at a village that I wanted to visit. I looked for a bridge but couldn't see one and I said to myself "*The river's too wide* to swim across so how do I get there?"

As I started to walk along the river bank, I noticed a young woman standing there and she seemed to look unhappy over something.

Again I thought to myself "*you're lonely and I'm lonely* so if I introduce myself I wonder if we could go out together sometime."

I walked up to her and as I did she said to another couple "*and this is my beloved.*" And that's when I woke up.

In the last part of the dream I never saw the female's face at all. I can't dance at all so that dream never made sense to me and I put it down to something that I had for supper that evening, the warm night and the excitement of seeing my parents again."

Sam said "Very interesting. Nancy how about you? Have you had any encounters at all?"

"Over the years, I have never had that *oh lonesome me* feeling, even before the children came and when Bob was away. I always felt as if I had someone watching over me.

When I was *sweet Lorraine's* age, I had an invisible dog that kept me company. Yes, we would talk sometimes and he would answer me in my head but most of the time he would just sit and wag his tail while I was talking.

I used to go over to the park and say goodbye to the birds when they sang their *September Song* but once Frank was born, my dog friend disappeared.

Oh, what it seemed to be for me was

that I was lonely as the only child then?

As Frank began to grow up and the arrival of Albert, I knew that *everybody loves somebody* and that *somebody loves me* now. Remember that I was young then and didn't know about the different kind of love I have now.

Yes Bob, *you brought a new kind of love to me* and because of it, *you make me feel so young* every day.

When your lover has gone away on a business trip, you miss them at first and feel as if a part of you is missing and then a few days later *the goin's great*. When Bob returned home, I felt as if I was completely whole again.

A few times when he has come home I have felt as if I have *one foot in heaven*. "*That's how much I love you*." said Nancy while she was looking at Bob.

Nancy then continued "like I told Dean the other day, I talk to God and ask for his help and I usually get it in one way or another.

The night that Dean had asked me the question about speaking to angels, I felt so frazzled that I told Bob that "*I'm gonna sit right down and write myself a letter.*"

I was sitting in the kitchen writing myself notes, not a letter, to remind me what was done, what was left to do and if I needed to get any more shopping.

For a few moments I heard a voice in my head and I thought I saw the same man at my kitchen window.

The voice said "Don't worry; everything is going to be great. You will learn a lot of new things from your family and you will find that you all have something in common.

You will never have to sing a *September Song* or say *shoo, shoo baby* because you are so *easy to love* by everybody. *I'll follow my secret heart* and be by your side always. *I'll be seeing you* again, because *I'll know* when you will need me." and that's when Bob walked into the kitchen for a glass of water.

Like I said, it was only a few moments that I heard the voice but it was very comforting for me.

I went to bed and felt as if the weight of the world had been taken off my shoulders and the tension of getting everything done before your arrivals had disappeared."

Sam looked at everyone individually. Put his elbows on his knees, cradled his chin in his hands and just said "MMM".

The look on his face was as if he was deep in thought but he was hesitant to say anything.

Rose said "Yes, that was very interesting indeed. Now I know what the man with the umbrella meant when he told me many years ago that he and his kind would always watch over me and my family.

I'll tell you all, my story now.

It was during my travels before I met Sam that I began seeing and hearing from the angels again.

I was just about to say goodnight to Irene at her front gate when we saw a fella with an umbrella walking down the street.

I never thought of him again until a

few years later when I was in France, in the 2020 Club.

I heard this voice say "Hey there." and turned to see; who I thought was Irene, who I hadn't seen for years. Irene was not there but the fella with an umbrella was standing there handing me some chips and quite adamantly suggested in a whispering voice "*hey won't you play your favorite number for the next five games.*"

I did and I won enough money to leave France and to visit Albert in Rome, before I was coming back home.

I was going to Rome via Vento when that old devil moon decided to upset my travel plans.

Accidents will happen at any time; however, I don't believe in accidents. I believe that everything happens for a reason.

My friend Delores left me stranded when she met some other friends of hers who were in Sammy's March for freedom.

I knew that *every time we say goodbye*, she would always end up in trouble but

I still decided not to go with her.

A few days later, I heard that someone called the sweetheart of Signa Chi had the group arrested and deported.

That night the fella with the umbrella came to me from out of nowhere while I was walking home.

He told me "You'll never walk alone because I'm walking behind you and *all of me* and my kind will always watch over you and your family.

You have never believed that *you're nobody until somebody loves* you because *when you're smiling,* you bring love and joy to everyone around you.

When you see the Lamplighters Serenade sign and you hear the coffee song *you're gonna love yourself* and someone special who will provide you the good life the way that you want to live it."

He was right because that was when I met Sam and instead of visiting Albert and coming home, I told Sam that "*I'll string along with you* to South America."

I loved it down in South America and

decided to stay there for a while.

No one could *call me irresponsible* because I knew that I would never be short of finances because I could always find work; even if it was selling *Candy Kisses* somewhere.

I got a job as a waitress at the *Birth Of The Blues* Coffee Shop and a studio type apartment in Monterey.

A week later, Sam went home to Cusco. I missed him and his weird sense of humour and *it came upon a midnight clear,* just after I had got home from work that I asked myself "*Which way did my heart go?*

I knew that I liked Sam very much, but was I in love with him?

It wasn't easy to carry on *with a song in my heart,* especially *when your lover has gone* and you know that you may never see him again. There had been other romances along the way, but with Sam, I felt so different.

It happened in Monterey about six weeks later.

It was my day off and I was just

leaving my studio when I bumped into Sam, and I mean bumped into Sam.

He had realized that he was in love with me and came back looking for me.

He couldn't find me as I had changed jobs and he thought that I had come home. I left the *Birth Of The Blues* Coffee Shop once I found out that it was a front for criminal activities and got a job at *That's Amore* Travel Agency. If I had to work on a weekend, I usually got a day off during the week.

We went for a coffee and started talking. When the waitress came over to our table, Sam ordered the two coffees and a small cake and as the waitress was walking back to the coffee machine, he called out to her "You had better make that two cakes; one for me and *one for my baby* here."

We saw each other every day after that and on *some enchanted evening*, Sam confessed to me "*You're in my heart* and *you do something to me. I've got you under my skin* in a bad way and *I only have eyes for you*.

I think *I dream of you* some nights. *I got the sun in the morning* but *I can't give you anything but love* at the moment but would you consider becoming my wife.

All of me will always be true to you *and when I die* you will never want for anything. I will have to teach you a few customs and the language of my town if you agree to marry me and come back with me."

My reply was "*You do something to me* too and *I only have eyes for you* as well, so my answer is yes.

When you have finished your units at the university, I will gladly go home with you because your country is good for my *body and soul*.

I can keep working at the travel agents till then and learn as much as I can about the industry. That way, if I save as much as I can and learn as much as I can, I'll be able to help you start your business.

What sort of travel business would you like to start?

When he told me that he wanted to

take tourists on short stay trips to the local places of interest, I knew that it would not be the *Wham! Bam! Thank You Mam* sort of business; and *what kind of fool am I* if I think I could be happy with someone who isn't honest.

We got married once he had finished his degree and had moved back to his home town. I am not sorry at all that I have married Sam and the man with the umbrella was right when he told me that I would have a special someone who would give me the good life that I want to live.

It has taken me awhile to learn both Spanish and Quechua properly but what I have and who I have in my life has made it all worthwhile.

Yes dad, you can still call me your rambling Rose; however, I don't do it so much now because I have the girls to look after.

Twice a year we take them to Machu Picchu to visit some friends there and to make sure that the people who house our tourists are happy with our service.

If either of our girls starts talking about seeing many discs in the sky, they are talking about UFO sightings as they are a common sight down there.

Oh, I am not saying that we see them every day but we do see them often.

The first one I saw was just after I had had Inka and I was *walking my baby back home* from the local store.

Both of our girls are quite open and not fazed when talking about the discs or angels or even having talked to them and getting messages from them.

It is all natural down home. In fact the man with the umbrella approached both Inka and Stella the day before we left and gave Inka this message "What you are thinking is right and you will learn what he meant when we are on holidays.

He also told me that I would be like you and would learn more than anyone can but I would always be safe and that I would always have someone to watch over me.

He told Stella that she would be a star in years to come and would help many people. You and papa will be very proud of her.

He turned to Nasha and told her to tell her mama that Huahuqui and Chasqui are here and she would understand it and explain it to everyone.

Inka told me "I didn't see him until he spoke to me and I didn't see him go and all I remember of him is his nice smile and his blue eyes because he was standing in front of a big white light.

Who is he mama and how did he know we lived here? Could he be one of those people from out of this world?"

Talking about messages; don't you think that it's time for you to give me an explanation about the message that Nasha's mama tried to tell me the day before we left?"

Sam sat back upright in his chair and said "It looks like I will have to now, after hearing all your stories.

Before I start, does anyone want another hot drink and something to eat?

I know that I could do with a very strong coffee."

SAM'S STORY

Before I tell you my story, I will explain to you why our girls believe in and are not fazed by UFOs and angels.

"Many thousands of years ago, the Inka people settled in Peru and lived around Machu Picchu, Cusco and the Inka Trail and spoke only in their own dialect of Quechua.

It is said that during the Huayara (Fertility Festival) the Acllacuna (chosen women) would stay a week with the Mamacuna (Mother Superior) and the Vilac Uma (the High Priest) in a Hauca (Sacred Place).

Every day they would make an Apachita (sacred offering), eat Canca (sacred bread) and drink Chicha (a fermented beverage, corn beer) out of an aquilla (golden goblet).

The hauasipascuna (the left out girls) would be sent out to look for the Napa (white albino llama) on the Pampa (the low level treeless grassy plain) just below the mountain range.

One evening a disc flew over the mountain range and it is believed that it landed just behind the mountain range that overlooked the Pampa (the low level treeless grassy plain).

In the morning whilst the hauasipascuna (the left out girls) were looking for the Napa (white albino llama), they saw a male and a female sitting by the tocco (the cave mouth).

It is believed that the male told them in their heads where they could find a Napa (white albino llama).

After they had taken the Napa (white albino llama) back to the place where the Mamacuna (Mother Superior) and the Vilac Uma (the High Priest) were staying, the hauasipascuna (the left out girls) were questioned on how they were able to find a Napa (white albino llama) so easily and quickly, when in many other years no-one else could find one.

The hauasipascuna (the left out girls) told them that the Sinchi (Chief Leader) had told them in their heads where to go.

"There were many Napa (white albino

llama)" said one of the hauasipascuna (the left out girls).

They were questioned again about the two people they saw and if they were approached by them on the Pampa (the low level treeless grassy plain).

One of the hauasipascuna (the left out girls) replied "Yes. The Sinchi (Chief Leader) was just like a puric (an able adult man) with blonde hair, a beautiful smile and *angel eyes*. He seemed to be surrounded in a shimmering light."

The Mamacuna (Mother Superior) and the Vilac Uma (the High Priest) was so pleased with the hauasipascuna (the left out girls) that they invited them to join in the celebrations and make an Apachita (sacred offering), eat Canca (sacred bread) and drink Chicha (a fermented beverage, corn beer) out of an aquilla (golden goblet) but not in the Hauca (Sacred Place).

The Acllacuna (chosen women) became angry and jealous and snuck out one morning and climbed the mountain to the tocco (the cave mouth) where they found a Yacarca (Soothsayer) sitting just outside drinking from a quero (wooden goblet).

It is believed that the Sinchi (Chief Leader) and the Yacarca (Soothsayer) took all but two of the Acllacuna (chosen women) into the cave.

The two Acllacuna (chosen women) who were left outside the cave were given messages and sent back down the mountain and back to the Mamacuna (Mother Superior).

The only part of the messages that the women could recall at the time was "The Yacarca (Soothsayer) will be watching over the valley and *in the still of the night* on *some enchanted evening* will go down to the plain and move all the Napa (white albino llama) to another safe place.

The Sinchi (Chief Leader) will also come on *some enchanted evening* at a different time to her and will visit one or two people in the villages around the Inka Trail.

No-one will ever know *where or when* he will visit because discs will be seen flying into and out of the mountains of Machu Picchu quite often.

If the Sinchi (Chief Leader) and I come back and we want people to know, then we will leave the message that Huahuqui (Supernatural Guardian Brother) and Chasqui (Messenger/Relay Runner) are here.

We will usually visit the *young at heart,* no matter what age they are first. We may show up at anytime and anywhere to anyone who needs us. Sinchi (Chief Leader) says "*As long as she needs* me or if he is in trouble, I will be there."

Usually he knows who needs him and when.

Rose, it was hard for me to tell you that, because you are not of my people.

It is a custom of my people to verbally hand down the stories of the past to our families when the child reaches the age of ten. It is said that the child will be of the level of understanding to take it all in.

In the past fifty years, Huahuqui (Supernatural Guardian Brother) has been called by his English name of

Earth Angel David by many people because more foreign tourists now visit Peru.

And that is why I started my Travel Agency so the tourist could visit where the discs come in and if they are lucky, Earth Angel David might visit with them."

Everyone was quiet for a few moments, trying to take in what Sam had just told them when Albert asked "If most of the others have had contact with this Earth Angel David, as you called him, why haven't Bob, Shannon and I been visited or heard anything from him?

And have you been visited by him?

Oh, I think that may have been a stupid question."

Sam replied "It was not a stupid question. Yes, David has visited me but there are quite a few people in my local area that haven't been visited by anyone like him at all.

Didn't you say earlier that when the lady helped you from the rope bridge that an unusual blonde haired man who walked past said "*Luck be a lady* and *anything goes* in life. Life, yes, she's funny that way but she will always be good to you. It's *just one of those things,* which you have to get through night and day, *nevertheless,* pennies from heaven will always fall your way."

Now think about this man and what he looked like?

Maybe there is a reason that he hasn't visited Bob or Shannon and maybe he never will."

Sylvia looked at Sam and said "Now I would like to hear your story."

Fred said "Yes, so would I and I would especially like to hear your version on how you met and tamed my rambling Rose?"

Sam said "As you are all aware of, I was born in Cusco and have grown up in and around the area.

Even though I have my own faith, I still believe in angels and other beings and how can I not when there are sightings of discs/UFOs seen quite regularly.

It's all right with me if my girls grow up believing what I believe, they will not be afraid of seeing, hearing or knowing that unusual things are happening.

I went to school and decided to go to University to study Archaeology but my studies changed direction in the second half of my second year.

I found that many tourists came to Peru and often tried to find guides to take them to all the different places of interest. They often wanted to go to Machu Picchu because they had heard that that was where there were many sightings of UFOs.

I thought that this was a great opportunity for me to start my own business for tour guides of the special places of interest.

I still get a thrill in visiting these places and I have also given some of the locals a chance to earn some money by housing tourists for about a week each month.

When I started my third year at the Cusco University, I knew that by changing to the travel side of my degree, I would have to finish it at the University in Monterey.

I decided to do some travelling and see a bit of the world before I started my Travel Agency so that I would be able to understand the different ways of life in different countries.

I had been in Rome for just over two weeks when I first saw Rose sitting at the café. I went back every day just to see if she was there and she was. I wanted to meet her but was unsure of how to go about it and then one day I plucked up the courage to do it.

Rose has already told you what happened after that but what she didn't tell you was that the girl that I was going steady with, left her home town to go to a Finishing School in Paris.

I asked her to *send me the pillow that you dream on* so that I could take it back to her and we could start seeing each other again but she told me that she wanted to go to Paris with no attachments except for her family.

I was heartbroken and it was then that I decided it was time to head home to continue my studies in Monterey.

Rose and I travelled to Monterey and during those few weeks together *all of me* knew that *you make me feel so young* and when *you go to my head you are my lucky star.*

I went home for a few weeks and it was then that I knew that *you taught me to love again* and that's when I came back looking for you.

You was just so beautiful, and still are, and the woman I wanted to share the rest of my life with because *you made me love you* by your *personality* and your wacky sense of humour.

When I arrived in Monterey and I couldn't find her, I naturally thought that she had gone back home to the States and *I wondered who's kissing her now* but it was just by chance that she actually bumped into me as she was coming out of her apartment block.

Rose do you remember what you said after I ordered those two cakes; you know when I told the waitress that one was for me and *one for my baby* here?

Rose chuckled to herself and replied "Didn't I say something like Hush, if you keep talking like that; *people will say we're in love* and you shouldn't say things like that *just for fun."*

Fred looked at Rose and then back to Sam and asked "How did you tame her and get her to marry and go into business with you?"

Sam replied "We had plenty of time to talk about our future and what we wanted from life and it seemed that we both had similar ideas.

The best thing is that I never had to ask Rose to *send me the pillow you dream on.* I am not saying that Rose and I don't have our differences, because we do and in the beginning we had some really big differences.

I knew that *something's gotta give* but I didn't know if we could make it through, but we did.

One day before we got married. I saw Rose with another male and for the first time in my life, I became jealous.

I approached her and said "*You belong*

to me and *yours is my heart alone.* Don't you sing me your *September song* so *love me or leave me?*

Make up your mind as to whom you want to be with?"

Well; I saw a side of Rose that I would never want to see again and I deserved it, because the male I saw her with was a friend and a teacher who was going to help her learn the more intricate parts of running a Travel Agency.

Young; foolish, was what I was that day. I know that some of *these foolish things* that we do, we learn by them and I have learned never to say *love me or leave me* but to say *love me, love me* instead; and it works better.

To tell you the truth; *I got the sun in the morning* most days but really *I don't care if the sun don't shine* because the love of Rose, Inka and my little *Stella by starlight* plus my work makes me very happy and contented."

Rose said "We call Stella that sometimes because on the night she was born, the sky was full of stars and there had also been the sighting of two discs landing that day.

When Sam proposed to me and said *"I can't give you anything but love."* I told him that *that's what I want from you* but he has given me much, much more than he knows and I am glad that he has enlightened me on some of his family history tonight."

Nancy said "I know that today has been a busy day for all of us and this evening has been very strange and informative.

It seems that in some way we have all been given messages and maybe *just one more chance* to get our lives to where we wanted them to be or to where our lives are at the moment.

Albert; Antonio asked about a church; well, there is one just two block north of here. I don't know about the rest of you but I think that I would like to go to church in the morning, *how about you?"*

Albert looked at Marie, who had a big smile on her face, and nodded yes. He then said "Well, Marie, the children and I will come with you."

In the end the whole family had agreed to go to church with Nancy in the morning.

Nancy, Louise and Sylvia were in the kitchen when Stella walked through the door rubbing her eyes and said "*I got the sun in the morning* so it means I have to get up and have my breakfast."

Louise bent down and picked her up saying "Come here you *embraceable you. I get a kick out of you* when you *hold me* and give me a kiss on the cheek.

Now what would you like for breakfast?"

Just as she said that, the four younger boys came into the kitchen together and told her what each of them wanted, and it was all different.

After breakfast was eaten and the kitchen tidied Antonio said "Well who's coming to church with us? *I feel a song coming on* or rather a Christmas carol."

"*I'll string along with you.*" said John, "that is if it's alright with you."

"*It's all right with me.*" replied Antonio "so let's go."

As they were walking home after church Shannon was talking to Dean and said "That hippie girl *Sunflower* whispered to me in church "We are leaving for Ohio tomorrow but I've got to tell you that *I've got a crush on you* and *I've got you under my skin. I dream of you* some nights but *what kind of fool am I* if I think that we could be anything more than friends at our age. May you and your family have a merry Christmas?"

Dean laughed and replied "Well at least she is leaving for good tomorrow. Imagine what it would be like for you at school if she stayed. She might be running around after you saying "*What now my love;* do you want me to get you a drink or something?"

Romeo said "It's a pity she's leaving 'cos you could have gotten her to do your homework for you."

Shannon mumbled "I knew that I shouldn't have told you. By the time you've finished spreading it around, you're going to make it sound like the *lady is a tramp.*

She is a really nice person and very brainy. In fact, *what kind of fool am I* or would I be; the teachers would know if she did my homework for me. I am the last person that I thought she would like as more than just a school friend. Come on, I'll race you home."

There were eight very excited children who ran through the front door of Nancy's house and each of them raced into the living room to see if Santa had left them any presents.

Julie suggested that they take off their coats and shoes and have a drink before they received their gifts.

John was given the job of playing Santa and giving out the gifts. He was told to make sure that he gave the boys the gifts from their grandparents at the same time so that they could open them together.

Romeo was the first to open his and called out to his parents "Papa, mama, look at what I've got. The two games that I was saving for; the Birth Of The Blues Gang and Now *Who's Got The Action.*"

Dean excitedly said "Thank you grandma and grandpa. My friend Justin has these games and I have wanted to get them but they sell out so quickly.

Mom, look I have those games De Camptown Races Heist and Long Ago And Far Away Space Invaders that I've wanted."

Bob said "We won't be seeing you now. Just remember that you do have school, homework and chores to do and most importantly, we do have guests here that you shouldn't ignore."

Antonio smiled as he opened his present and went over and gave his grandparents a hug. "Grazie." he said "I love Western Movies and now I have *Who's Sorry Now* Western and Wogon Wheels Rodeo. Both of these have been advertised over in Italy and I have wanted to get them."

Dean asked Shannon what he got and he replied "That Old Black Magic and *Ghost Riders In The Sky.*"

Louise gave her grandfather the book that she had bought in London and told him that it was a great story as she had already finished her copy.

"Please tell a little about the book but *please don't tell me how the story ends* as that would spoil the reading of it." said Fred.

Sylvia was surprised by her gift from her husband. It too was a book, "*If you are but a dream.*"

She looked at her husband and said "You've borrowed this book from the library last year and when I went to borrow it, I was told that it had accidentally been destroyed in a house fire.

I know that you told me a bit about it and that it was a very good story but *please don't tell me how the story ends.*

I will wait until I get home before I read it as I want to spend as much time with my family as I can while they're here all together."

Just as the last of the gifts were being opened, the family heard *strange music* coming from the kitchen that made them all get up and investigate.

On the table were five light blue envelopes; each with a family's name on it.

The inquisitive children of each respective family gathered around their parents anxiously waiting for them to open their envelopes to see what was inside.

They all opened their envelopes at the same time and when Bob opened his, he showed Nancy the contents and said "Sam, Rose, thank you, but you shouldn't have. You have already given us our gifts."

Rose's other siblings and her parents all said the same thing after showing each other what was inside their envelopes.

Rose questioningly asked "What are you thanking Sam and me for. We don't know anything about these envelopes."

"Come on." said Albert "how could you not know about them? It's a three week all-expense paid trip to Machu Picchu, Cusco and the Sacred Valley."

Sam replied "Rose is telling you the truth. We don't know anything about them. You know that we were the first to leave the kitchen when we got home from church and you also know that neither of us has left the living room."

He then looked in his own envelope and showed Rose its contents; a three week all-expense paid trip to Hawaii.

There was also an accompanying note which read "Your belief, faith and love for your families is something rare in these days.

You do not need to go to a place where your faith will be strengthened, so you are going to a place where both of you have secretly wanted to visit.

You never told each other of this secret because you felt that it would not be viable; however when it is time to go, you will find that your friends and work colleagues will support and help you.

Your two wonderful daughters will learn much about the Hawaiian culture and will enjoy the holiday immensely.

Last night was *some enchanted evening* for me and my kind and we enjoy being *riders in the sky*.

Have a merry Christmas and remember that *I'll be seeing you* again because I am always with you and your family."

Marie took the envelope from Albert's hand and looked inside to find a similar note that read "The holiday will give you an interesting break where you will learn a great amount and will strengthen your faith.

The memories of your trip will remain with your children for as long as they live. I will know when you are there and I will arrange for you to see a disc fly into the Machu Picchu Mountains.

Hearing you talk about your experiences last night left me *with a song in my heart. I don't care if the sun shine* is only on the *silver bells* because Marie you will always say in so many different ways, "One for me and *one for my baby* here." and it will also include your husband.

Your husband is very *dedicated to you* and your children.

I only have eyes for you and your family at this time but I will be with you and your family *all the way* through the rest of yours and their lives.

Enjoy your holiday and have a merry Christmas."

Bob heard a voice in his head that said "You haven't read your note yet? You had a dream that hasn't come true because *lucky be a lady* is not needed. *So far* you have shown more love and thoughtfulness to your family and those around you.

You could have let your employees leave and to sort out their own solutions for themselves.

What makes the sunset beautiful for some people; the thoughtfulness of other people like you. There are at least three families rejoicing tonight because of the decisions you have made over the past year and they will always be loyal to you.

When you *begin the Beguine,* you start a beautiful dance and you and your family's lives will always be like that dance.

Once you have read your notes I will make any memory of the coming holidays disappear from the children's minds until you are actually there."

"Bob, Bob." said Nancy "What is it? Are you going to read our note out to us?"

Sam looked at Bob's face and said "You heard someone talking to you, didn't you?"

Bob looked at Sam as he handed the note to Nancy and said "Yes I did. He told me that the dream I had many years ago has not come true as it was not needed. He told me that the decisions that I have made in the past year were right and that the three families were rejoicing tonight."

Nancy read their note "It was on *some enchanted evening* when a family was together and the secret truths were told.

Love is the tender trap that nearly everyone gets caught up in but it is how they react to what is happening that makes the world of difference. *They say it's wonderful* to be in love but occasionally *something's gotta give*.

You and Nancy were always able to work through the issues as they arose and never did either of you have to say *love or leave me*.

The holiday will give you an interesting break where you will learn a great amount and will strengthen your faith.

The memories of your trip will remain with your children for as long as they live.

I will know when you are there and I will arrange for you to see a disc fly into the Machu Picchu Mountains. Shannon will never be a full believer as he has an analytical mind for most things."

Fred opened his note and said "*Here goes*. My note reads. "You and Sylvia should be very proud of yourselves for raising your four wonderful children. You have given so much of your lives to your children and your community and you deserve a reward. *You make me feel so young* every time I visit you and Sylvia.

It seems that both of you are the more *embraceable you* and that is why *it's always you* that people want to talk to especially when they need some advice.

You have both been visited by me in the past and the holiday will give you an interesting break where you will learn a great amount and will strengthen your faith.

The memories of your trip will remain with you for as long as you live and you will both enjoy long lives together. I will know when you are there and I will arrange for you to see a disc fly into the Machu Picchu Mountains.

Over the years neither of you had to worry *when your lover has gone* away for short periods of time.

You always used to tell the other one "I'll carry on *just as though you were here* so *lover come back to me* as soon as you can. The love and the trust that you have in each other is *too marvelous for words*.

You did *begin the beguine* for each of your children and they will carry on the dance and will pass it on for many generations to come."

"Well, I guess that it only leaves us to read our note." said Julie.

Frank opened his note and began reading it "I was hoping that you would be last to read your note because there is something in it for all of your family.

John and Louise are so much older than the others and I have not left them out of having the holiday with you; however, it may be just be a little more difficult to organize a time when you are all free at the same time.

The holiday will give you an interesting break where you will learn a great amount and will strengthen your faith.

The memories of your trip will remain with your children for as long as they live. I will know when you are there and I will arrange for you to see a disc fly into the Machu Picchu Mountains.

Bob you can never say "*I'm always chasing rainbows.*" because you always seem to be several steps ahead of them.

I still get a thrill watching you handle tricky situations and the times that you need help, you gladly accept it.

There are at least three families rejoicing tonight because of the decisions you made in London and they will always be loyal to you.

If I only had a match for every couple like you, then there would be more peace and less heartache by people singing the *September song* and saying "*love me or leave me.*" in the world today.

Julie, you always make sure that you *powder your face* with sunshine every day so everyone will feel happy. *You make me feel so young* and I go around *with a song in my heart.*

I don't know *what became of me* during the early years of your life but I knew that *something's gotta give* and it did.

Instead of you becoming a bitter person as you were growing up; you have grown into a beautiful, strong woman with a healthy and steadfast marriage.

You have given so much more than you received when you were young. *You do something to me* that you will never understand.

My kind cannot interfere with a person's free will and we only have unconditional love for everything;

however, there are some individuals who do make us want to work harder for them and you are one of them.

John, the *more I see you,* the more I am certain that you will become as successful as your father.

The girl you knew in France will not stay there because she will marry a gentle man and move to Australia where she will be happy.

You will marry a girl who will support you and will often say to you "Never *let me go lover. These things I offer you,* my love, my heart, my trust and support are all I have to give you."

You will continue to know when you are in danger but you will never be afraid.

Louise, you are another *embraceable you* that many people will want to know and you will never *sway* from being who you are. No matter who you are with, you will always say "*I've gotta be me.*"

I do not know *where or when* you will meet your *lover* but he will be a good man.

You will never want for anything or fear hearing him sing the *September song*.

That is all I have to say to you for the time being but *I'll be seeing you some other time* in the future.

Enjoy your holiday in Peru."

"Albert, Albert." shouted a scared Marie "are you alright, you have just gone so pale like all the statues at home."

"Oh yes, I'm alright. Look to see if each of your notes are signed with a "D" now." said Albert.

They all looked at their notes and saw in the bottom right hand corner a letter "D".

"That wasn't there when I read our note a minute ago." said Sam. "Albert what just happened a minute ago?"

Albert was slow in replying "I heard a voice that said to look in the corner because he forgot to sign the notes with his initial and I saw the face of a blonde hair man smiling at me and it seemed as if he was also smiling at me through his blue eyes."

"*Hey won't you play* with me and my

glow worm?" called Stella to Lorraine.

"All right, and I can play with my glow worm too? I called mine sweet Louise cos she called me *sweet Lorraine*. Have you got a name for yours yet?" answered Lorraine.

"I don't know yet. I might call it Wormy or maybe Baby. If I call it baby and I'm playing with it, I can ask mama for some cake and when she gives me just one piece, I can ask for more cos I'll say I want one for me and *one for my baby.*" said Stella.

Inka walked up behind Stella and said "That won't work. Mama is smarter than we are and you know that we are only allowed one piece of cake each."

"*Hey won't you play* one of your games Antonio and then we can all play one of our games afterwards. If we watch you, then if you need help, we might be able to help you." said Dean.

"I know that it's wrong for me to say this, but sometimes *I get a kick out of you* when you are struggling to work out how the game is played." said Romeo.

After the two weeks were over, the respective families that visited went home.

During that year, each family took their holidays and those who went to Peru were not disappointed.

They visited many places, learned a lot and as promised saw a disc flying into the Machu Picchu Mountains.

Shannon still is not a full believer even though he saw a UFO.

Sam and Rose along with their daughters enjoyed their holiday in Hawaii where Rose fell pregnant again. Her son was born in Cusco and he looked like Sam.

Don't ever think that you are alone, because you're not. Not everyone believes in angels and UFOs but everyone does have their faith, even if they say they don't.

People will tell you not to believe everything that you read but just remember that angels may exist and visit people who need them during their lives.

It could happen to you one day when you are in need; a voice in your head telling you the solution to an issue or it may be just a warm loving feeling that comforts you.

REFERENCE

VERY BEST OF THE RAT PACK CD
COME FLY WITH ME
AIN'T THAT A KICK IN THE HEAD
TOO CLOSE FOR COMFORT: - SAMMY
DAVIS JR
I'VE GOT YOU UNDER MY SKIN
WHO'S GOT THE ACTION?
A LOT OF LIVIN' TO DO
RING-A-DING DING
EEE-O ELEVEN: - SAMMY DAVIS JR
LUCK BE A LADY
VOLARE (NEL BLU DIPINTO DI BLU)
BIRTH OF THE BLUES: - SAMMY
DAVIS JR
WITCHCRAFT
YOU'RE NOBODY 'TIL SOMEBODY
LOVES YOU
I GET A KICK OUT OF YOU
SAM'S SONG: - SAMMY DAVIS JR.
& DEAN MARTIN
I'M GONNA LIVE UNTIL I DIE
ALTERNATE VERSION
EVERYBODY LOVES SOMEBODY

ME AND MY SHADOW: - FRANK SINATRA
& SAMMY DAVIS JR.

RAT PACK CD

BLUE SKIES: - FRANK SINATRA
SATURDAY NIGHT IS THE LONELIEST
NIGHT OF THE WEEK: - FRANK SINATRA
SWEET LORRAINE: - FRANK SINATRA
I'VE GOT A CRUSH ON YOU: - FRANK
SINATRA
IF I EVER LOVE AGAIN: - FRANK
SINATRA
LOVER: - FRANK SINATRA
WHEN YOU'RE SMILING: - FRANK
SINATRA
APRIL IN PARIS: - FRANK SINATRA
TRY A LITTLE TENDERNESS: - FRANK
SINATRA
THAT OLD BLACK MAGIC: - FRANK
SINATRA
THE BROOKLYN BRIDGE: - FRANK
SINATRA
BODY AND SOUL: - FRANK SINATRA
IF I ONLY HAD A MATCH: - FRANK
SINATRA
S'POSIN': - FRANK SINATRA

AUTUMN IN NEW YORK: - FRANK
SINATRA
LONDON BY NIGHT: - FRANK SINATRA
NEVERTHELESS: - FRANK SINATRA
CHATTANOOGIE SHOE SHINE BOY: -
FRANK SINATRA
THE HUCKLEBUCK: - FRANK SINATRA
ALL OF ME: - FRANK SINATRA
STORMY WEATHER: - FRANK SINATRA
ONE FOR MY BABY: - FRANK SINATRA
YOU DO SOMETHING TO ME: - FRANK
SINATRA
AMERICAN BEAUTY ROSE: - FRANK
SINATRA
WHAT I'VE GOT IN MIND: - SAMMY
DAVIS JNR
MENTION A MANSION: - SAMMY
DAVIS JNR
YOU'RE GONNA LOVE YOURSELF (IN THE
MORNING): - SAMMY DAVIS JNR
SMOKE, SMOKE, SMOKE (THAT
CIGARETTE): - SAMMY DAVIS JNR
OH LONESOME ME: - SAMMY
DAVIS JNR
WE COULD HAVE BEEN THE CLOSEST OF
FRIENDS: - SAMMY DAVIS JNR

HEY WON'T YOU PLAY (ANOTHER SOMEBODY DONE): - SAMMY DAVIS JNR

PLEASE DON'T TELL ME HOW THE STORY ENDS: - SAMMY DAVIS JNR

THE RIVER'S TOO WIDE: - SAMMY DAVIS JNR

WHAT KIND OF FOOL: - SAMMY DAVIS JNR

OUT OF THIS WORLD: - SAMMY DAVIS JNR

HERE I'LL STAY: - DEAN MARTIN

TILL THEN: - DEAN MARTIN

ABOUT A QUARTER TO NINE: - DEAN MARTIN

MEMORY LANE: - DEAN MARTIN

HOLD ME: - DEAN MARTIN

I GOT THE SUN IN THE MORNING: - DEAN MARTIN

ALL OF ME: - DEAN MARTIN

OH MARIE: - DEAN MARTIN

WHICH WAY DID MY HEART GO: - DEAN MARTIN

TAKES TWO TO TANGO: - DEAN MARTIN

EVERYBODY LOVES SOMEBODY: - DEAN MARTIN

ON A SLOW BOAT TO CHINA: - DEAN
MARTIN
THE GLOW WORM: - DEAN MARTIN
RAMBLING ROSE: - DEAN MARTIN
I'LL STRING ALONG WITH YOU: - DEAN
MARTIN

50 ORIGINAL RECORDINGS CD - IMPORT

THAT OLD BLACK MAGIC
I GET A KICK OUT OF YOU: - FRANK
SINATRA
MEMORIES ARE MADE OF THIS: - DEAN
MARTIN
EASY TO LOVE: - SAMMY DAVIS, JR.
LET ME GO LOVER: - DEAN MARTIN
YOU MAKE ME FEEL SO YOUNG: - FRANK
SINATRA
LOVE & MARRIAGE: - FRANK SINATRA
STANDING ON THE CORNER: - DEAN
MARTIN
JUST ONE MORE CHANCE: - DEAN
MARTIN
IT'S ALL RIGHT WITH ME: - SAMMY
DAVIS, JR.
YOUNG & FOOLISH: - DEAN MARTIN

THE BIRTH OF THE BLUES: - SAMMY DAVIS, JR.
A FOGGY DAY (IN LONDON TOWN): - FRANK SINATRA
LONESOME ROAD: - SAMMY DAVIS, JR.
SPOKEN FOR: - SAMMY DAVIS, JR.
OLD DEVIL MOON: - FRANK SINATRA
ME 'N' YOU 'N' THE MOON: - DEAN MARTIN
FRANKIE & JOHNNIE: - SAMMY DAVIS, JR.
MAKIN WHOOPEE: - FRANK SINATRA
YOU BROUGHT A NEW KIND OF LOVE TO ME: - FRANK SINATRA
WHO'S SORRY NOW: - DEAN MARTIN
WHEN YOU'RE SMILING: - DEAN MARTIN
HOW ABOUT YOU?: - FRANK SINATRA
GLAD TO BE UNHAPPY: - SAMMY DAVIS, JR.
BECAUSE OF YOU: - SAMMY DAVIS, JR.
THAT'S AMORE
TOO CLOSE FOR COMFORT: - SAMMY DAVIS, JR.
I'VE GOT YOU UNDER MY SKIN: - FRANK SINATRA
KISS: - DEAN MARTIN

SOMEONE TO WATCH OVER ME: - FRANK SINATRA
SWAY: - DEAN MARTIN
SOMETHING'S GOTTA GIVE: - SAMMY DAVIS, JR.
SEPTEMBER SONG: - SAMMY DAVIS, JR.
PENNIES FROM HEAVEN: - FRANK SINATRA
YOU BELONG TO ME: - DEAN MARTIN
HEY THERE: - SAMMY DAVIS, JR.
TOO MARVELLOUS FOR WORDS: - FRANK SINATRA
INNAMORATA: - DEAN MARTIN
MAMBO ITALIANO: - DEAN MARTIN
LOVE ME OR LEAVE ME: - SAMMY DAVIS, JR.
ALL OF YOU: - SAMMY DAVIS, JR.
SOUTH OF THE BORDER: - FRANK SINATRA
IT HAPPENED IN MONTEREY: - FRANK SINATRA
THE NAUGHTY LADY OF SHADY LANE: - DEAN MARTIN
MONEY BURNS A HOLE IN MY POCKET: - DEAN MARTIN

MY FUNNY VALENTINE: - SAMMY DAVIS, JR.
AND THIS IS MY BELOVED: - SAMMY DAVIS, JR.
YOU'RE GETTING TO BE A HABIT WITH ME: - FRANK SINATRA
ONCE IN LOVE WITH AMY: - DEAN MARTIN
BYE, BYE BLACKBIRD: - DEAN MARTIN

STARS THAT MADE LOS VEGAS CD - IMPORT

ON THE SUNNY SIDE OF THE STREET: - FRANK SINATRA
DOLORES: - FRANK SINATRA
SOME ENCHANTED EVENING: - DEAN MARTIN
HEY WON'T YOU PLAY: - SAMMY DAVIS, JR.
EMBRACEABLE YOU: - FRANK SINATRA
TAKE YOUR GIRLIE TO THE MOVIES: - DEAN MARTIN
SEPTEMBER SONG: - DEAN MARTIN
FOOLS RUSH IN: - FRANK SINATRA
I'LL BE SEING YOU: - FRANK SINATRA
SUNFLOWER: - DEAN MARTIN

OH LONESOME ME: - SAMMY
DAVIS, JR.
GHOST RIDERS IN THE SKY: - DEAN
MARTIN
IMAGINATION: - FRANK SINATRA
RIVER'S TOO WIDE: - SAMMY
DAVIS, JR.
FIVE FOOT TWO EYES OF BLUE: -
SAMMY DAVIS, JR.
JUST FOR YOU: - DEAN MARTIN
STORMY WEATHER: - FRANK SINATRA
DREAMER: - DEAN MARTIN
PLEASE DON'T TELL ME HOW THE
STORY ENDS: - SAMMY DAVIS, JR.
I DREAM OF YOU: - FRANK SINATRA
I CAN'T GIVE YOU ANYTHING BUT LOVE:
- DEAN MARTIN
TIME AFTER TIME: - FRANK SINATRA
WON'T BE SATISFIED UNTIL YOU BREAK
MY HEART: - DEAN MARTIN
SWEET LORRAINE: - FRANK SINATRA
MONEY SONG: - DEAN MARTIN
THAT'S HOW MUCH I LOVE YOU: -
FRANK SINATRA
FAR AWAY PLACES: - DEAN MARTIN
COFFEE SONG: - FRANK SINATRA

SOMEONE LIKE YOU: - DEAN MARTIN
SATURDAY NIGHT: - FRANK SINATRA
NOW IT LIES NOW IT LIES NOW IT LIES:
- DEAN MARTIN
SO FAR: - FRANK SINATRA
I GOT THE SUN IN THE MORNING: -
DEAN MARTIN
THEY SAY IT'S WONDERFUL: - FRANK
SINATRA
SAULT STE MARIE: - DEAN MARTIN
ROAD TO MANDALAY: - FRANK SINATRA
ROOM FULL OF ROSES: - DEAN MARTIN
STELLA BY STARLIGHT: - FRANK
SINATRA
THROUGH A LONG SLEEPLESS NIGHT: -
DEAN MARTIN
YOU'LL NEVER WALK ALONE: - FRANK
SINATRA

**ON THE SUNNY SIDE OF THE STREET
CD - IMPORT**
ON THE SUNNYSIDE OF THE STREET
DOLORES
SOME ENCHANTED EVENING
HEY WON'T YOU PLAY
EMBRACEABLE YOU

TAKE YOUR GIRLIE TO THE MOVIES
SEPTEMBER SONG
FOOLS RUSH IN
I'LL BE SEEING YOU
OH, LONESOME ME
SUNFLOWER
GHOST RIDERS IN THE SKY
IMAGINATION
THE RIVERS TOO WIDE
FIVE FOOT TWO, EYES OF BLUE
JUST FOR FUN
STORMY WEATHER
DREAMER
PLEASE DON'T TELL ME HOW THE
STORY ENDS
I DREAM OF YOU

RAT PACK-THE BIG THREE CD - IMPORT

I'VE GOT YOU UNDER MY SKIN
OLD DEVIL MOON
HOW ABOUT YOU?
LOVE AND MARRIAGE
JEEPERS CREEPERS
DANCING ON THE CEILING
A FOGGY DAY

I'VE GOT THE WORLD ON A STRING
YOU MAKE ME FEEL SO YOUNG
MAKIN' WHOOPEE
TAKING A CHANCE ON LOVE
SOMEONE TO WATCH OVER ME
I GET A KICK OUT OF YOU
YOU BROUGHT A NEW KIND OF
LOVE TO ME
SWINGIN' DOWN THE LANE
ANYTHING GOES
WHAT IS THIS THING CALLED LOVE?
YOUNG AT HEART
IT HAPPENED IN MONTEREY
TOO MARVELLOUS FOR WORDS
HEY, BROTHER, POUR THE WINE
MEMORIES ARE MADE OF THIS
THE NAUGHTY LADY OF SHADY LANE
WHEN YOU'RE SMILING
YOUNG AND FOOLISH
YOU BELONG TO ME
THATS AMORE
KISS
STANDING ON THE CORNER
MAMBO ITALIANO
WHO'S SORRY NOW?
JUST ONE MORE CHANCE

SWAY
POWDER YOUR FACE WITH SUNSHINE
(SMILE! SMILE! SMILE!)
LET ME GO LOVER
ONCE IN LOVE WITH AMY
MONEY BURNS A HOLE IN MY POCKET
I DONT CARE IF THE SUN DONT SHINE
WHAM! BAM! THANK YOU MA'AM
HOW D' YA LIKE YOUR EGGS IN THE
MORNING?
BE-BOP THE BEGUINE
SOMETHING'S GOTTA GIVE
IT'S ALL RIGHT WITH ME
LOVE ME OR LEAVE ME
BIRTH OF THE BLUES
THAT OLD BLACK MAGIC
MY FUNNY VALENTINE
YOU DO SOMETHING TO ME
BODY AND SOUL
THESE FOOLISH THINGS

ULTIMATE COLLECTION CD - IMPORT

THAT OLD BLACK MAGIC: - SAMMY
DAVIS, JR.
THAT'S AMORE: - DEAN MARTIN

ONE FOR MY BABY (ONE MORE FOR THE ROAD): - FRANK SINATRA
POWDER YOUR FACE: - DEAN MARTIN
APRIL IN PARIS: - FRANK SINATRA
JUST FOR FUN: - DEAN MARTIN
HEY THERE: - SAMMY DAVIS, JR.
BYE BYE BABY: - FRANK SINATRA
YOU BELONG TO ME: - DEAN MARTIN
YOU DO SOMETHING TO ME: - FRANK SINATRA
YOU GO TO MY HEAD: - FRANK SINATRA
HOW DO YOU SPEAK TO AN ANGEL: - DEAN MARTIN
ALL OF YOU: - SAMMY DAVIS, JR.
UNDER THE BRIDGES OF PARIS: - DEAN MARTIN
IT ALL DEPENDS ON YOU: - FRANK SINATRA
MEMORIES ARE MADE OF THIS: - DEAN MARTIN
ONCE IN LOVE WITH AMY: - FRANK SINATRA
LOVE OR LEAVE ME: - SAMMY DAVIS, JR.
SWAY: - DEAN MARTIN
SHOULD I (REVEAL): - FRANK SINATRA

LET ME GO LOVER: - DEAN MARTIN
MY FUNNY VALENTINE: - SAMMY
DAVIS, JR.
WHO'S SORRY NOW: - DEAN MARTIN
BODY AND SOUL: - FRANK SINATRA
THERE'S MY LOVER: - DEAN MARTIN
AS YOU ARE: - DEAN MARTIN
I AM LOVED: - FRANK SINATRA
MY HEART HAS FOUND A NEW HOME
NOW: - DEAN MARTIN
BLUE SKIES: - FRANK SINATRA
BIRTH OF THE BLUES: - SAMMY
DAVIS, JR.
SOMETHING'S GOTTA GIVE: - SAMMY
DAVIS, JR.
IN THE COOL COOL COOL OF THE
EVENING: - DEAN MARTIN
WHEN YOU'RE SMILING: - FRANK
SINATRA
THESE FOOLISH THINGS: - FRANK
SINATRA
UNTIL YOU LOVE SOMEONE: - DEAN
MARTIN
EASY TO LOVE: - SAMMY DAVIS, JR.
TRY A LITTLE TENDERNESS: - FRANK
SINATRA

THAT LUCKY OLD SIN: - DEAN MARTIN
I'VE GOT A CRUSH ON YOU: - FRANK
SINATRA
SOME ENCHANTED EVENING: - FRANK
SINATRA
LUNA MEZZO MARE: - DEAN MARTIN
VIENI SU (SAY YOU LOVE ME TOO): -
DEAN MARTIN
LOVER: - FRANK SINATRA
AND THIS IS MY BELOVED: - SAMMY
DAVIS, JR.
BECAUSE OF YOU: - SAMMY DAVIS, JR.
KISS: - DEAN MARTIN
BEGIN THE BEGUINE: - SAMMY
DAVIS, JR.
SIX BRIDGES TO CROSS: - SAMMY
DAVIS, JR.
BE HONEST WITH ME: - DEAN MARTIN
I'M GONNA PAPER ALL MY WALLS WITH
YOUR LOVE LETTERS: - DEAN MARTIN

RAT PACK - ALWAYS CD - IMPORT
WHAT I'VE GOT IN MIND
AS TIME GOES BY
YOU BELONG TO ME
COME SUNDOWN

BOP! GOES MY HEART
BECAUSE YOU'RE MINE
THE SONG IS YOU
HEY, WON'T YOU PLAY
THE LADY LOVES TO DANCE
I FALL IN LOVE TO EASILY
YOU'RE GONNA LOVE YOURSELF (IN
THE MORNING)
MUSKAT RAMBLE
ALWAYS
WE COULD HAVE BEEN THE CLOSET
OF FRIENDS
THERE'S NO BUSINESS LIKE SHOW
BUSINESS
THE PEANUT VENDOR
SMOKE, SMOKE, SMOKE (THAT
CIGARETTE)
I'M GONNA PAPER ALL MY WALLS WITH
YOUR LOVE LETTERS
PENNIES FROM HEAVEN
WHAM! BAM! THANK YOU MAM!

LEGENDARY RAT PACK CD - IMPORT
'S WONDERFUL: - SINATRA
SOLITAIRE: - DEAN MARTIN
COME SUNDOWN: - SAMMY DAVIS JNR

WHAT I'VE GOT IN MIND: - SAMMY DAVIS JNR

I'VE GOT LOVE TO KEEP ME WARM: - FRANK SINATRA

I RAN ALL THE WAY HOME: - DEAN MARTIN

IT'S A LOVELY DAY TOMMOROW: - FRANK SINATRA

BLUE SMOKE (KOHU-AUWAHI): - DEAN MARTIN

MENTIONA MANSION: - SAMMY DAVIS JNR

THE LAMPLIGHTERS SERENADE: - FRANK SINATRA

NEVER BEFORE: - DEAN MARTIN

YOU'RE GONNA LOVE YOURSELF (IN THE MORNING): - SAMMY DAVIS JNR

SOMEBODY LOVES ME: - FRANK SINATRA

OH BOY! OH BOY! OH BOY! OH BOY! OH BOY!: - DEAN MARTIN

SMOKE, SMOKE, SMOKE, (THAT CIGARETTE): - SAMMY DAVIS JNR

TENDERLY: - FRANK SINATRA

MY HEART HAS FOUND A HOME NOW: - DEAN MARTIN

OH LONESOME ME: - SAMMY
DAVIS JNR
I DONT KNOW WHY: - FRANK SINATRA
WHEN YOUR SMILING: - DEAN MARTIN

RAKISH & RAMPANT CD
CD1
DEAN MARTIN:
HEY BROTHER POUR THE WINE
MEMORIES ARE MADE OF THIS
THE NAUGHTY LADY OF SHADY LANE
YOUNG ; FOOLISH
THAT'S AMORE
KISS
MAMBO ITALIANO
WHO'S SORRY NOW?
SWAY
POWDER YOUR FACE WITH SUNSHINE
LET ME GO LOVER
MONEY BURNS A HOLE IN MY POCKET
I DON'T CARE IF THE SUN DON'T SHIN
WHAM BAM! THANK YOU MA'AM
HOW D'YA LIKE YOUR EGGS IN THE...
FRANK SINATRA:
I'VE GOT YOU UNDER MY SKIN
OLD DEVIL MOON

HOW ABOUT YOU?
JEEPERS CREEPERS
DANCING ON THE CEILING
CD2
FRANK SINATRA:
I'VE GOT THE WORLD ON A STRING
YOU MAKE ME FEEL SO YOUNG
MAKIN' WHOOPEE
TAKING A CHANCE ON LOVE
I GET A KICK OUT OF YOU
YOU BROUGHT A NEW KIND OF
LOVE TO.
SWINGIN' DOWN THE LANE
ANYTHING GOES
WHAT IS THIS THING CALLED LOVE
YOUNG AT HEART
SAMMY DAVIS JR:
BE-BOP THE BEGUIN
SOMETHING'S GOTTA GIVE
LOVE ME OR LEAVE ME
THAT OLD BLACK MAGIC
YOU DO SOMETHING TO ME
HEY THERE SEE
EASY TO LOVE
ALL OF YOU
COME RAIN OR SHINE

SMILE DARN YA SMILE

STARS IN LAS VEGAS: 200 FAMOUS TRACKS CD

I'LL BE SEEING YOU: - (WITH FRANK SINATRA)
THE SUNSHINE OF YOUR SMILE
SHAKE DOWN THE STARS
EAST OF THE SUN
TRADE WINDS
OUR LOVE AFFAIR
YOU AND I SEE ALL
HOU ABOUT YOU
YOU MIGTH HAVE BELONGED TO ANOTHER
TAKE ME
LET'S GET AWAY FROM IT ALL
DAYBREAK
PEOPLE WILL SAY WE'RE IN LOVE
WITHOUT A SONG
FOOL RUSH IN
THERE ARA THINGS
I DON'T STAND A GHOST OF A CHANCE
TELL ME AT MIDNIGTH
OH! LOOK AT ME NOW
DEVIL MY CARE

BLACK COFFEE: - (WITH SARAH
VAUGHAN)
AS YOU DESIRE ME
WHILE YOU ARE GONE
JUST FRIENDS
YOU TAUGHT ME TO LOVE AGAIN
LONELY GIRL
YOU'RE MINE, YOU
THE NEARNESS OF YOU
I'M CRAZY TO LOVE YOU
DON'T BE AFRAID
I'LL KNOW
THINKING OF YOU
THESE THING I OFFER YOU
AFTER HOURS
JUST A MOMENT MORE
TIME TO GO
CORNER TO CORNER
STREET OF DREAMS
I CONFESS
A BLUES SERENADE
EVERYTHING I HAVE IS YOURS: -
(WITH BILLY ECKSTINE)
FOOLS RUSH IN (WERE ANGELS
FEAR TO TREAD)
MR. B'S BLUES

SOMEHOW
CARAVAN
BODY AND SOUL
I'VE NEVER BEEN IN LOVE BEFORE
AS LONG AS I LIVE
I LEFT MY HAT IN HAITI
HERE COMES THE BLUES

RAT PACK - BOY'S NIGHT OUT CD
HERE GOES
WHO'S GOT THE ACTION
YES I CAN
WE OPEN IN VENICE
YOU CAN'T LOVE 'EM ALL
OL'MACDONALD
THERE IS NOTHIN' LIKE A DAME
GRAZIE, PREGO, SCUSI
THE BOYS' NIGHT OUT
THE GOIN'S GREAT
GUYS AND DOLLS
SOMETHINGS'S GOTTA GIVE
BABY-O
RIVER, STAY 'WAY FROM MY DOOR
(LOVE IS) THE TENDER TRAP
ALL IN A NIGHT'S WORK
JUST ONE OF THOSE THINGS

ONCE IN A LIFETIME
GUYS & DOLLS
20 20

RAT PACK - SEPTEMBER SONG CD
I'VE GOT YOU UNDER MY SKIN
THE BIRTH OF THE BLUES
NATURE BOY
SOME ENCHANTED EVENING
HEY,THERE
GOODNIGHT IRENE
I'LL ALWAYS LOVE YOU
SEPTEMBER SONG
I'M A FOOL TO WANT YOU
NEVERTHELESS (I'M IN LOVE WITH
YOU)
CHICAGO
ON A CLEAR DAY YOU CAN SEE
FOREVER
GHOST RIDERS IN THE SKY
MAM'SELLE
SPINNING WHEEL
JUST FOR FUN
THE GOOD LIFE
HEART AND SOUL

RAT PACK - BEST OF CD - IMPORT

THAT'S AMORE: - DEAN MARTIN
EVERYBODY LOVES SOMEBODY: - DEAN MARTIN
MEMORIES ARE MADE OF THIS: - DEAN MARTIN
THAT LUCKY OLD SUN: - DEAN MARTIN
ON A SLOW BOAT TO CHINA: - DEAN MARTIN
BABY IT'S COLD OUTSIDE: - DEAN MARTIN
ALL OF ME: - DEAN MARTIN
WALKIN' MY BABY BACK HOME: - DEAN MARTIN
DON'T LET THE STARS GET IN YOUR EYES: - DEAN MARTIN
I DON'T CARE IF THE SUN DON'T SHINE: - DEAN MARTIN
I'LL STRING ALONG WITH YOU: - DEAN MARTIN
IF: - DEAN MARTIN
I GOT THE SUN IN THE MORNING: - DEAN MARTIN
IF YOU WERE THE ONLY GIRL IN THE WORLD: - DEAN MARTIN
SEPTEMBER SONG: - DEAN MARTIN

VOLARE/ON AN EVENING IN ROMA: -
DEAN MARTIN
I WONDER WHO'S KISSING HER NOW: -
DEAN MARTIN
I CAN'T GIVE YOU ANYTHING BUT LOVE:
- DEAN MARTIN
YOU'RE NOBODY TILL SOMEBODY LOVES
YOU: - SAMMY DAVIS, JR.
CHICAGO: - SAMMY DAVIS, JR.
ONE FOR MY BABY (AND ONE MORE FOR
THE ROAD): - SAMMY DAVIS, JR.
WHAT KIND OF FOOL AM I: - SAMMY
DAVIS, JR.
I'M ALWAYS CHASING RAINBOWS: -
SAMMY DAVIS, JR.
ON A CLEAR DAY: - SAMMY DAVIS, JR.
I'VE GOTTA BE ME: - SAMMY
DAVIS, JR.
FOLKS WHO LIVE ON A HILL: - SAMMY
DAVIS, JR.
MORE I SEE YOU/THE SECOND TIME
AROUND: - SAMMY DAVIS, JR.
IF MY FRIENDS COULD SEE ME NOW: -
SAMMY DAVIS, JR.
I HAVE DREAMED: - SAMMY
DAVIS, JR.

AS LONG AS SHE NEEDS ME: - SAMMY DAVIS, JR.
BIRTH OF THE BLUES: - SAMMY DAVIS, JR.
WITH A SONG IN MY HEART: - SAMMY DAVIS, JR.
WHAT NOW MY LOVE: - SAMMY DAVIS, JR.
IMPOSSIBLE DREAM: - SAMMY DAVIS, JR.
PLEASE DON'T TALK ABOUT ME WHEN I'M GONE: - SAMMY DAVIS, JR.
EVERY TIME WE SAY GOODBYE: - SAMMY DAVIS, JR.
WHEN YOU'RE SMILING: - FRANK SINATRA
BEGIN THE BEGUINE: - FRANK SINATRA
ALL OF ME: - FRANK SINATRA
THESE FOOLISH THINGS: - FRANK SINATRA
WE KISS IN A SHADOW: - FRANK SINATRA
ONE FOR MY BABY (AND ONE MORE FOR THE ROAD): - FRANK SINATRA
SOME ENCHANTED EVENING: - FRANK SINATRA

NANCY: - FRANK SINATRA
BLUE SKIES: - FRANK SINATRA
APRIL IN PARIS: - FRANK SINATRA
SEPTEMBER SONG: - FRANK SINATRA
THE OLD BLACK MAGIC: - SINATRA, THE, FRANK
WHERE OR WHEN: - FRANK SINATRA
NIGHT AND DAY: - FRANK SINATRA
TRY A LITTLE TENDERNESS: - FRANK SINATRA
I'VE GOT A CRUSH ON YOU: - FRANK SINATRA
STORMY WEATHER: - FRANK SINATRA
IF I COULD WRITE A BOOK: - FRANK SINATRA
AUTUMN IN NEW YORK: - FRANK SINATRA
BYE BYE BABY: - FRANK SINATRA

RAT PACK - ON STAGE CD - IMPORT
DRINK TO ME ONLY WITH THINE EYES /
I DON'T CARE IF THE SUN SHINE / I
LOVE VEGAS
JUNE IN JANUARY (MARTIN)
VIA VENETO (MARTIN)
ON AN EVENING IN ROME (MARTIN)

VOLARE (NEL BLU DIPINTO DI BLU)
(MARTIN)
I ONLY HAVE EYES FOR YOU (SINATRA)
MY HEART STOOD STILL (SINATRA)
PLEASE BE KIND (SINATRA)
CALL ME IRRESPONSIBLE (SINATRA)
LUCK BE A LADY
AT THE SALAD BAR (SINATRA/MARTIN)
KIDDIE ALBUM MEDLEY
(SINATRA/MARTIN): - SAMMY DEAN &
FRANK (DAVIS JR.)
LADY IS A TRAMP, THE (DAVIS JR.)
ROCK-A-BYE YOUR BABY (DAVIS JR.)
SAMMY'S MARCH (DAVIS JR.)
GUYS & DOLLS (SINATRA/MARTIN)
OLDEST ESTABLISHED, THE
(PERMANENT FLOATING CRAP GAME IN
NEW YORK): - (SINATRA/MARTIN)
INTRODUCING THE BAND
(SINATRA/MARTIN)
RING-A-DING-DING (INSTRUMENTAL)
JOHNNY CARSON INTRODUCES DEAN
MARTIN (NOT USED IN STORY)
SEND ME THE PILLOW THAT YOU
DREAM ON (MARTIN)
KING OF THE ROAD (MARTIN)

EVERYBODY LOVES SOMEBODY
(MARTIN)
VOLARE/ON AN EVENING IN ROMA
(MARTIN)
JOHNNY CARSON INTRODUCES SAMMY
DAVIS JR. (DAVIS JR.) (NOT USED IN
STORY)
MY SHINING HOUR (DAVIS JR.)
WHO CAN I TURN TO (DAVIS JR.)
I'VE GOT YOU UNDER MY SKIN / YOU
CAME A LONG WAY FROM ST. LOUIS /
HIT THE ROAD JACK / YOU ARE MY
SUNSHINE /
BEE BOM ONE FOR MY BABY
JOHNNY CARSON INTRODUCES FRANK
SINATRA (NOT USED IN STORY)
GET ME TO THE CHURCH ON TIME
(SINATRA)
FLY ME TO THE MOON (SINATRA)
LUCK BE A LADY (SINATRA)
I ONLY HAVE EYES FOR YOU (SINATRA)
I'VE GOT YOU UNDER MY SKIN
(SINATRA)
PLEASE BE KIND (SINATRA)
YOU MAKE ME FEEL SO YOUNG
(SINATRA)

MY KIND OF TOWN (SINATRA)
BIRTH OF THE BLUES / CLOSING TUNE -
(STUDIO)

VERY BEST OF CD - IMPORT
MEMORIES ARE MADE OF THIS: - DEAN
MARTIN
LOVE AND MARRIAGE: - FRANK SINATRA
THE BIRTH OF THE BLUES: - FRANK
SINATRA
THAT OLD BLACK MAGIC: - SAMMY
DAVIS JR
SOMEONE TO WATCH OVER ME: -
SAMMY DAVIS JR
SANTA LUCIA: - DEAN MARTIN
CHATANOOGIE SHOE SHINE BOY: -
FRANK SINATRA
WALKIN' MY BABY BACK HOME: - DEAN
MARTIN
I'LL NEVER SMILE AGAIN: - FRANK
SINATRA
THE GYPSY IN MY SOUL: - SAMMY
DAVIS JR
WHEN YOU'RE SMILING: - DEAN MARTIN
THE HUCKLEBUCK: - FRANK SINATRA
LAURA: - SAMMY DAVIS JR

POWDER YOUR FACE WITH SUNSHINE: - DEAN MARTIN

S' WONDERFUL: - FRANK SINATRA

WHO'S SORRY NOW: - DEAN MARTIN

CAN'T YOU SEE I'VE GOT THE BLUES: - SAMMY DAVIS JR

ON THE SUNNY SIDE OF THE STREET: - FRANK SINATRA

LET ME GO LOVER: - DEAN MARTIN

LOVE IS THE TENDER TRAP: - FRANK SINATRA

IN THE WEE SMALL HOURS OF THE MORNING: - FRANK SINATRA

PLEASE DON'T TALK ABOUT ME WHEN I'M GONE: - SAMMY DAVIS JR

THAT LUCKY OLD SUN (JUST ROLLS AROUND HEAVEN ALL DAY): - DEAN MARTIN

AMERICAN BEAUTY ROSE: - FRANK SINATRA

YOU AND YOUR BEAUTIFUL EYES: - DEAN MARTIN

DEDICATED TO YOU: - SAMMY DAVIS JR

EMBRACEABLE YOU: - FRANK SINATRA

STORMY WEATHER: - FRANK SINATRA

BIRTH OF THE BLUES: - SAMMY
DAVIS JR
I GOT THE SUN IN THE MORNING: -
DEAN MARTIN
MY FUNNY VALENTINE: - SAMMY
DAVIS JR
SOLITAIRE: - DEAN MARTIN
FULL MOON AND EMPTY ARMS: - FRANK
SINATRA
SOMETHING'S GOTTA GIVE: - SAMMY
DAVIS JR
LEARNIN' THE BLUES: - FRANK SINATRA
THE NAUGHTY LADY OF SHADY LANE: -
DEAN MARTIN
SAME OLD SATURDAY NIGHT: - FRANK
SINATRA
BYE BYE BLACKBIRD: - DEAN MARTIN
I AIN'T GOT NOBODY: - SAMMY
DAVIS JR
ALL OF YOU: - SAMMY DAVIS JR

ULTIMATE RATPACK CD - IMPORT
LOVE ; MARRIAGE
YOUNG ; FOOLISH
HEY THERE
THE TENDER TRIP

UNDER THE BRIDGES OF PARIS
AND THIS MY BELOVED
SAME OLD SATURDAY NIGHT
THAT'S AMORE
THE MAN WITH THE GOLDEN ARM
YOU BELONG TO ME
SOUTH OF THE BORDER
THAT'S WHAT I WANT FROM YOU
THE GYPSY IN MY SOUL
MY BLUE HEAVEN
IN NAPOLI
MELODY OF LOVE
I'LL KNOW
LOVE ME LOVE ME
BEGIN THE BEGUINE
SMILE DARN YA SMILE
IN LOVE
LOVE IS ALL THAT MATTERS
I'M WALKING BEHIND YOU
AS LONG AS SHE NEEDS ME
COME BACK TO SORRENTO
ALL THE THINGS YOU ARE
I THINK ILIKE YOU
ALL I HAVE TO GIVE TO YOU
IF I LOVE YOU
THE FOLKS WHO LIVE ON THE HILL

WHAT COULD BE MORE BEAUTIFUL
WHAT'LL I DO?
EVERYTIME WE SAY GOODBYE
TWO SLEEPY PEOPLE
I ONLY HAVE EYES FOR YOU
I'M GLAD THERE IS YOU
MOMENTS LIKE THIS
A GHOST OF A CHANCE
TOMORROW WITH ME
I'D CRY LIKE A BABY
APRIL IN PARIS
JUST THE HITS
SWAY
LEARNIN' THE BLUES
SOMETHING'S GOTTA GIVE
YOUNG AT HEART
MAMBO ITALIANO
LOVE ME OR LEAVE ME
LET ME GO LOVER

FAR AWAY PLACES CD - IMPORT
ONE FOR MY BABY
YOU BELONG TO ME
DAY BY DAY
DON'T LET THE STARS GET IN
YOUR WAY

STELLA BY STARLIGHT
BYE, BYE, BLACKBIRD
EVERYBODY LOVES SOMEBODY
THAT'S HOW MUCH I LOVE YOU
FAR AWAY PLACES
ALL OF ME
LONELY IS THE NAME
SOMEONE LIKE YOU
SATURDAY NIGHT
HOW IT LIES, HOW IT LIES, HOW IT
LIES
SO FAR
I GTO THE SUN IN THE MORNING
THEY SAY IT'S WONDERFUL
OH MARIE

**RAT PACK - DEAN MARTIN FRANK
SINATRA SAMMY DAVIS CD -
IMPORT**
STORMY WEATHER
ONE FOR MY BABY
YOU DO SOMETHING TO ME
AMERICAN BEAUTY ROSE
WHAT I'VE GOT IN MIND
MENTION A MANSION
OH LONESOME ME

YOU'RE GONNA LOVE YOURSELF (IN THE
MORNING)
SMOKE, SMOKE, SMOKE (THAT
CIGARETTE)
WE COULD HAVE BEEN THE CLOSEST
OF FRIENDS
HEY WON'T YOU PLAY
PLEASE DON'T TELL ME HOW THE
STORY ENDS
THE RIVER'S TOO WIDE
WHAT KIND OF FOOL
OUT OF THIS WORLD
HERE I'LL STAY
TILL THEN
ABOUT A QUARTER TO NINE
MEMORY LANE
HOLD ME

FRANK SINATRA-DEAN MARTIN CD - IMPORT

DEAN MARTIN / I LEFT MY HEART IN
SAN FRANCISCO
DEAN MARTIN / I'M GONNA SIT RIGHT
DOWN AND WRITE MYSELF A LETTER
DEAN MARTIN / ON AN EVENING IN
ROMA

FRANK SINATRA / GOODY GOODY
FRANK SINATRA / CHICAGO
FRANK SINATRA / WHEN YOUR LOVER
HAS GONE
FRANK SINATRA / PLEASE BE KIND
FRANK SINATRA / YOU'RE NOBODY
TILL SOMEBODY LOVES YOU
SAMMY DAVIS JR. / WHAT KIND OF
FOOL AM I
SAMMY DAVIS JR. / OUT OF THIS
WORLD
SAMMY DAVIS JR. / SHE'S FUNNY
THAT WAY
SAMMY DAVIS JR. / HEY THERE

RAT PACK VOL. 3-THE RAT PACK CD - IMPORT
DISC 1

IF I LOVED YOU: - FRANK SINATRA
JOHNNY GET YOUR GIRL: - DEAN
MARTIN
EVERYTIME WE SAY GOODBYE: - SAMMY
DAVIS JNR
STELLA BY STARLIGHT: - FRANK
SINATRA
HAPPY FEET: - DEAN MARTIN

LET'S KEEP SWINGING: - SAMMY
DAVIS JNR
SUNDAY MONDAY OR ALWAYS: - FRANK
SINATRA
YOU AND YOUR BEAUTIFUL EYES: -
DEAN MARTIN
WICTHITA LINEMAN: - SAMMY
DAVIS JNR
I'LL NEVER SMILE AGAIN: - FRANK
SINATRA
PEG O MY HEART: - DEAN MARTIN
MY PERSONAL PROPERTY: - SAMMY
DAVIS JNR
CLOSE TO YOU: - FRANK SINATRA
SILVER BELLS: - DEAN MARTIN
ACCIDENTS WILL HAPPEN: - FRANK
SINATRA
DISC 2
WHAT MAKES THE SUNSET
WALKIN' MY BABY BACK HOME: - DEAN
MARTIN
SO FAR: - FRANK SINATRA
SANTA LUCIA: - DEAN MARTIN
YOU'D BETTER SIT DOWN KIDS: -
SAMMY DAVIS, JR.

A FELLOW NEEDS A GIRL: - FRANK
SINATRA
HOLD ME: - DEAN MARTIN
YES I CAN: - SAMMY DAVIS, JR.
THAT'S HOW MUCH I LOVE YOU: -
FRANK SINATRA
HAVE A LITTLE SYMPATHY: - DEAN
MARTIN
WHAT'S A KID LIKE YOU DOING IN A
PLACE LIKE THIS: - SAMMY DAVIS, JR.
YOU ARE LOVE: - FRANK SINATRA
JUST FOR FUN: - DEAN MARTIN
BEAUTIFUL THINGS: - SAMMY
DAVIS, JR.
A LITTLE BIRD TOLD ME: - FRANK
SINATRA
DISC 3
JUST ONE OF THOSE THINGS: - FRANK
SINATRA
I STILL GET A THRILL: - DEAN MARTIN
WHAT THE WORLD NEEDS NOW IS
LOVE: - SAMMY DAVIS JNR, BUDDY RICH
SOMEBODY LOVES ME: - FRANK
SINATRA
CANDY KISSES: - DEAN MARTIN

WHAT DID I HAVE THAT I DON'T
HAVE NOW
APRIL IN PARIS: - FRANK SINATRA
LET'S TAKE AN OLD FASHIONED WALK: -
DEAN MARTIN
WHAT BECAME OF ME: - SAMMY DAVIS
JNR, BUDDY RICH
LOVE ME OR LEAVE ME: - FRANK
SINATRA
SEPTEMBER SONG: - DEAN MARTIN
WE'LL BE TOGETHER AGAIN
SWEET LORRAINE: - FRANK SINATRA
DREAMER WITH A PENNY: - DEAN
MARTIN
AND WHEN I DIE
DISC 4
I STILL GET A THRILL: - FRANK SINATRA
WHAT THE WORLD NEEDS NOW IS
LOVE: - DEAN MARTIN
SOMEBODY LOVES ME: - SAMMY
DAVIS JNR
CANDY KISSES: - FRANK SINATRA
WHAT DID I HAVE THAT I DON'T HAVE
NOW: - DEAN MARTIN

TRIBUTE TO RAT PACK : TRIBUTE TO THE RAT PACK VOL. 2-TRIBUTE TO THE RAT PACK CD

MY HEART STOOD STILL
LONG AGO AND FAR AWAY: - FRANCK SINATRA
I FEEL A SONG COMING ON: - DEAN MARTIN
AREN'T YOU GLAND YOU'RE YOU: - FRANCK SINATRA
PLEASE DON'T TALK ABOUT ME WHEN I'M GONE
WHY WAS I BORN: - FRANCK SINATRA
POLKA DOTS AND MOONBEAMS: - FRANCK SINATRA
THE ONE I LOVE BELONGS TO SOMEBODY ELSE: - FRANCK SINATRA
THE COFFEE SONG: - FRANCK SINATRA
DEDICATED TO YOU: - SAMMY DAVIS, JR.
SHE'S FUNNY THAT WAY: - FRANCK SINATRA
THERE'S NO YOU: - FRANCK SINATRA
IT'S A LOVELY DAY TOMORROW: - FRANCK SINATRA
THAT'S AMORE: - DEAN MARTIN

I'VE GOT A CRUSH ON YOU: - FRANCK
SINATRA
COME RAIN OR COME SHINE: - FRANCK
SINATRA
VIOLETS FOR YOU FURS: - FRANCK
SINATRA
GUESS I'LL HANG MY TEARS OUT TO
DRY: - FRANCK SINATRA
EAST OF THE SUN WEST OF THE MOON:
- FRANCK SINATRA
STRANGE MUSIC: - FRANCK SINATRA
I DON'T STAND A GHOST OF A CHANCE
WITH YOU: - FRANCK SINATRA
YOU'RE BREAKING MY HEART ALL OVER
AGAIN: - FRANCK SINATRA
MY HEART TELLS ME
I ONLY HAVE EYES FOR YOU: - FRANCK
SINATRA
THESE FOOLISH THINGS: - FRANCK
SINATRA
SMILE DARN YA SMILE: - SAMMY
DAVIS, JR.
OH WHAT IT SEEMED TO BE: - FRANCK
SINATRA
SWEET LORRAINE: - FRANCK SINATRA
IT'S ALWAYS YOU: - FRANCK SINATRA

SHOO, SHOO BABY: - FRANCK SINATRA
THE MONEY SONG: - DEAN MARTIN
WITH A SONG IN MY HEART: - FRANCK
SINATRA
I'VE HAD FEELING BEFORE: - FRANCK
SINATRA
THE DAY AFTER FOREVER: - FRANCK
SINATRA
I GOT THE SUN IN THE MORNING: -
DEAN MARTIN
DREAMY BLUES: - SAMMY DAVIS, JR.
WAS THE LAST TIME I SAW YOU: -
FRANCK SINATRA
LOOKING FOR YESTERDAY: - FRANCK
SINATRA
CRADLE SONG: - FRANCK SINATRA
HEAD ON M Y PILLOW: - FRANCK
SINATRA
YOU'RE LONELY AND I'M LONELY: -
FRANCK SINATRA
AS TIE GOES BY: - FRANCK SINATRA
THE SKY FELL DOWN: - FRANCK
SINATRA
HERE COMES THE NIGHT
VIENI SU SAY YOU LOVE ME TOO: -
DEAN MARTIN

LOVE ME AS I AM: - FRANCK SINATRA
PUT YOUR DREAMS AWAY: - FRANCK SINATRA
THE FABLE OF THE ROSE: - FRANCK SINATRA
IF I LOVED YOU: - FRANCK SINATRA
GOT A GREAT BIG SHOVEL: - SAMMY DAVIS, JR.

TRIBUTE TO RAT PACK : TRIBUTE TO THE RAT PACK VOL. 1-TRIBUTE TO THE RAT PACK CD

DISC 1

LAST CALL FOR LOVE
ALL OF ME: - DEAN MARTIN
AMOR: - FRANCK SINATRA
FIVE MINUTES MORE: - FRANCK SINATRA
AZURE: - SAMMY DAVIS JR
DO YOU KNOW WHY
TOO ROMANTIC: - FRANCK SINATRA
YOU ARE MY LUCKY STAR: - SAMMY DAVIS JR
SEPTEMBER SONG: - FRANCK SINATRA
YOU BELONG: - DEAN MARTIN
SPEAK LOW: - FRANCK SINATRA

THAT OLD BLACK MAGIC: - FRANCK
SINATRA
NO LOVE NO NOTHING: - FRANCK
SINATRA
YOU GO TO MY HEAD: - FRANCK
SINATRA
IS YOU IS OR IS YOU AIN'T MY BABY: -
FRANCK SINATRA
I'M SORRY DEAR: - SAMMY DAVIS JR
THE NEARNESS OF YOU: - FRANCK
SINATRA
I BELIEVE: - FRANCK SINATRA
WHERE OR WHEN: - FRANCK SINATRA
THE WAY YOU LOOK TONIGHT: -
FRANCK SINATRA
OH MARIE: - DEAN MARTIN
DISC 2
YOURS IS MY HEART ALONE: - SAMMY
DAVIS JR
SHADOWS ON THE SAND: - FRANCK
SINATRA
MIGHTY LAK' A ROSE: - FRANCK
SINATRA
THAT OLD FEELING: - FRANCK SINATRA
LET ME LOVE YOU TONIGHT: - FRANCK
SINATRA

POWDER YOUR FACE WITH SUNSHINE
SMILE! SMILE! SMILE: - DEAN MARTIN
YOU MIGHT HAVE BELONGED TO
ANOTHER: - FRANCK SINATRA
BE-BOP THE BEGUINE: - SAMMY
DAVIS JR
NONE BUT THE LONELY HEART: -
FRANCK SINATRA
AND THEN YOU KISSED ME: - FRANCK
SINATRA
WHISPERING: - FRANCK SINATRA
STARDUST: - FRANCK SINATRA
COME BACK TO SORRENTO TORN A
SURRIENTO: - DEAN MARTIN
THERE ARE THING: - FRANCK SINATRA
IT COULD HAPPEN TO YOU: - FRANCK
SINATRA
I'LL NEVER SMILE AGAIN: - FRANCK
SINATRA
DON'T FORGET TONIGHT TOMORROW: -
FRANCK SINATRA
YOU WAS: - DEAN MARTIN
CLOSE TO YOU: - FRANCK SINATRA
FOOLS RUSH IN: - FRANCK SINATRA
INKA TINKA: - SAMMY DAVIS JR
I DON'T CARE IF THE SUN DON'T SHINE

PERSONALITY: - FRANCK SINATRA
APRIL PLAYED THE FIDDLE: - FRANCK SINATRA
NOT SO LONG AGO: - FRANCK SINATRA
MOMENTS IN THE MOONLIGHT: - FRANCK SINATRA
I COULDN'T SLEEP A WINK LAST NIGHT: - FRANCK SINATRA
IT NEVER ENTERED MY MIND: - FRANCK SINATRA
STORMY WEATHER: - FRANCK SINATRA

LIVE AND SWINGIN': THE RAT PACK LIVE AT THE VILLA VENICE DVD AUDIO
MEDLEY
MY KIND OF GIRL
I LEFT MY HEART IN SAN FRANCISCO
I'M GONNA SIT RIGHT DOWN AND WRITE MYSELF A LETTER
MEDLEY
GOODY GOODY
WHEN YOUR LOVER HAS GONE
MONOLOGUE
PLEASE BE KIND
ANGEL EYES

YOU'RE NOBODY TILL SOMEBODY
LOVES YOU
WHAT KIND OF FOOL AM I
OUT OF THIS WORLD
SHE'S FUNNY THAT WAY
HEY THERE
COMEDY
MEDLEY
MEDLEY
IMPRESSIONS
BIRTH OF THE BLUES
DANNY THOMAS INTRODUCTION (NOT
USED IN STORY)
NANCY (WITH THE LAUGHING FACE)
ME AND MY SHADOW
SAM'S SONG
BIRTH OF THE BLUES
ONE FOR MY BABY (AND ONE FOR THE
ROAD)

**BEST OF THE RAT PACK VOL. 1 MP3
ALBUM**
ON THE SUNNY SIDE OF THE STREET: -
FRANK SINATRA
DOLORES: - FRANK SINATRA
EMBRACEABLE YOU: - FRANK SINATRA

SOME ENCHANTED EVENING: - DEAN
MARTIN
HEY WON'T YOU PLAY: - SAMMY DAVIS
JR SAMMY DAVIS, JR.
TAKE YOUR GIRLIE TO THE MOVIES: -
DEAN MARTIN
SEPTEMBER SONG: - DEAN MARTIN
FOOLS RUSH IN: - FRANK SINATRA
I'LL BE SEEING YOU: - FRANK SINATRA
OH, LONESOME ME: - SAMMY DAVIS JR
SAMMY DAVIS, JR.
SUNFLOWER: - DEAN MARTIN
GHOST RIDERS IN THE SKY: - DEAN
MARTIN
IMAGINATION: - FRANK SINATRA
RIVER'S TOO WIDE: - SAMMY DAVIS JR
SAMMY DAVIS, JR.
EYE FOOT TWO, EYES OF BLUE: - DEAN
MARTIN
JUST FOR FUN: - DEAN MARTIN
STORMY WEATHER: - FRANK SINATRA
DREAMER: - DEAN MARTIN
PLEASE DON'T TELL ME HOW THE
STORY ENDS: - SAMMY DAVIS JR SAMMY
DAVIS, JR.
I DREAM OF YOU: - FRANK SINATRA

BEST OF THE RAT PACK VOL. 2 MP3 ALBUM

I CAN'T GIVE YOU ANYTHING BUT LOVE: - DEAN MARTIN

TIME AFTER TIME: - FRANK SINATRA

WON'T BE SATISFIED UNTIL YOU BREAK MY HEART: - DEAN MARTIN

SWEET LORRAINE: - FRANK SINATRA

MONEY SONG: - DEAN MARTIN

THAT'S HOW MUCH I LOVE YOU: - FRANK SINATRA

FAR AWAY PLACES: - DEAN MARTIN

COFFEE SONG: - FRANK SINATRA

SOMEONE LIKE YOU: - DEAN MARTIN

SATURDAY NIGHT: - FRANK SINATRA

HOW IT LIES, HOW IT LIES, HOW IT LIES: - DEAN MARTIN

SO FAR: - FRANK SINATRA

I GOT THE SUN IN THE MORNING: - DEAN MARTIN

THEY SAY IT'S WONDERFUL: - FRANK SINATRA

SAULT STE MARIE: - DEAN MARTIN

ROAD TO MANDALAY: - FRANK SINATRA

ROOM FULL OF ROSES: - DEAN MARTIN

STELLA BY STARLIGHT: - FRANK
SINATRA
THROUGH A LONG SLEEPLESS NIGHT: -
DEAN MARTIN
YOU'LL NEVER WALK ALONE: - FRANK
SINATRA

SAMMY DAVIS, JR / DEAN MARTIN / FRANK SINATRA - LIVE AND SWINGIN': THE ULTIMATE RAT PACK COLLECTION CD

FANFARE INTRODUCTION (NOT USED IN
STORY)
DRINK TO ME ONLY WITH THINE EYES /
WHEN YOU'RE SMILING / THE LADY IS A
TRAMP
I LEFT MY HEART IN SAN FRANCISCO
I'M GONNA SIT RIGHT DOWN AND
WRITE MYSELF A LETTER
VOLARE / ON AN EVENING IN ROMA
GOODY GOODY
CHICAGO
WHEN YOUR LOVER HAS GONE
MONOLOGUE
PLEASE BE KIND
WHAT KIND OF FOOL AM I

YOU'RE NOBODY TILL SOMEBODY
LOVES YOU
OUT OF THIS WORLD
SHE'S FUNNY THAT WAY
HEY THERE
COMEDY
BRAZIL / YOU ARE TOO BEAUTIFUL /
CECILIA (DOES YOUR MOTHER KNOW
YOU'RE OUT) / LOVE WALKED IN / YOU
MADE ME LOVE YOU
NOTHING COULD BE FINER / PLEASE BE
KIND / DANCING WITH TEARS IN MY
EYES / MARIA / TRY A LITTLE
TENDERNESS
SWING LOW SWEET CHARIOT / I CAN'T
GIVE YOU ANYTHING BUT LOVE / TOO
MARVELOUS FOR WORDS / PENNIES
FROM HEAVEN
A FOGGY DAY / EMBRACEABLE YOU /
THE LADY IS A TRAMP / WHERE OR
WHEN
IMPRESSIONS
BIRTH OF THE BLUES
DANNY THOMAS INTRODUCTION (NOT
USED IN STORY)
NANCY (WITH THE LAUGHING FACE)

ME AND MY SHADOW
SAM'S SONG
BIRTH OF THE BLUES
REPRISE

TRIBUTE TO RAT PACK : TRIBUTE TO THE RAT PACK VOL. 3-TRIBUTE TO THE RAT PACK CD
YOURS IN MY HEART
JUST AS THOUGH YOU WERE HERE: - FRANK SINATRA
SOME OTHER TIME: - FRANK SINATRA
OIMAN RIVER: - FRANK SINATRA
HERE LIES LOVE: - SAMMY DAVIS, JR.
TAKE ME: - FRANK SINATRA
HOMESICK THATS ALL: - FRANK SINATRA
THIS IS THE BEGINNING OF THE END: - FRANK SINATRA
IN THE COOL COOL COOL: - DEAN MARTIN
MY SHINING HOUR: - FRANK SINATRA
ALL THE THINGS YOU ARE: - FRANK SINATRA
IF LOVELINESS WERE MUSIC: - FRANK SINATRA

YOU AND I: - FRANK SINATRA
WALKIN MY BABY BACK HOME: - DEAN
MARTIN
THE GIRL THAT I MARRY: - FRANK
SINATRA
WHEN YOUR LOVER HAS GONE: - FRANK
SINATRA
BEGIN THE BEGUINE: - FRANK SINATRA
THE SUNSHINE OF YOUR SMILE: -
FRANK SINATRA
SAN FERNANDO VALLEY: - FRANK
SINATRA
LOVER COME BACK TO ME: - FRANK
SINATRA
WOGON WHEELS: - SAMMY DAVIS, JR.
ON A LITTLE STRET IN SINGAPORE
BLUE SKIES: - FRANK SINATRA
NANCY: - FRANK SINATRA
SATURDAY NIGHT: - FRANK SINATRA
YOU ARE TOO BEAUTIFUL: - FRANK
SINATRA
I AINT GOT NABODY: - SAMMY
DAVIS, JR.
HOW ABOUT YOU?: - FRANK SINATRA
TEA FOR TWO: - FRANK SINATRA
MAKE BELIEVE: - FRANK SINATRA

THE THINGS WE DID LAST SUMMER: - FRANK SINATRA
ILL BE SEEING YOU: - FRANK SINATRA
OUR LOVE AFFAIR: - FRANK SINATRA
LUNA MEZZO MARE: - DEAN MARTIN
ALL THIS AND HEAVEN TOO: - FRANK SINATRA
THE HOUSE I LIVE IN: - FRANK SINATRA
DEVIL MAY CARE: - FRANK SINATRA
IF YOU ARE BUT A DREAM: - FRANK SINATRA
WERE GONNA ROLL: - SAMMY DAVIS, JR.
TIME AFTER TIME: - FRANK SINATRA
IN THE BLUE OF THE EVENING: - FRANK SINATRA
WHERE DO YOU KEEP YOUR HEART?: - FRANK SINATRA
WE NEVER TALK MUCH: - DEAN MARTIN
I DONT CARE WHO KNOWS
KISS ME AGAIN: - FRANK SINATRA
NIGHT AND DAY: - FRANK SINATRA
WHEN YOURE SMILING: - DEAN MARTIN
SAY IT: - FRANK SINATRA
ILL FOLLOW MY SECRET HEART: - FRANK SINATRA

WHAT CAN I DO: - SAMMY DAVIS, JR.

FRANK SINATRA - CHRISTMAS WITH THE RAT PACK AND FRIENDS CD
JINGLE BELLS
IT CAME UPON A MIDNIGHT CLEAR
THE CHRISTMAS SONG
WHAT KIND OF FOOL AM I
O LITTLE TOWN OF BETHLEHEM
SILVER BELLS
WHERE OR WHEN
SANTA CLAUS IS COMING TO TOWN
ADESTE FIDELES
SILENT NIGHT
IN THE STILL OF THE NIGHT
GOD REST YE MERRY GENTLEMEN

DEAN MARTIN - CHRISTMAS WITH THE RAT PACK CD
LET IT SNOW! LET IT SNOW! LET IT SNOW!
MISTLETOE AND HOLLY
CHRISTMAS TIME ALL OVER THE WORLD
HARK THE HERALD ANGELS SING
SILVER BELLS
THE CHRISTMAS WALTZ

RUDOLPH THE RED NOSED REINDEER
JINGLE BELLS
HAVE YOURSELF A MERRY LITTLE
CHRISTMAS
PEACE ON EARTH/SILENT NIGHT
IT CAME UPON A MIDNIGHT CLEAR
WINTER WONDERLAND
THE CHRISTMAS SONG
THE FIRST NOEL
WHITE CHRISTMAS
I'LL BE HOME FOR CHRISTMAS (IF ONLY
IN MY DREAMS)

CHRISTMAS WITH THE RAT PACK
MP3 ALBUM

I'VE GOT MY LOVE TO KEEP ME WARM: -
DEAN MARTIN
MISTLETOE AND HOLLY: - FRANK
SINATRA
CHRISTMAS TIME ALL OVER THE
WORLD: - SAMMY DAVIS, JR.
FIRST NOEL: - FRANK SINATRA
BABY, IT'S COLD OUTSIDE: - DEAN
MARTIN
I BELIEVE: - FRANK SINATRA
SILVER BELLS: - DEAN MARTIN

CHRISTMAS SONG: - SAMMY DAVIS, JR
HARK! THE HERALD ANGELS SING: -
FRANK SINATRA
RUDOLPH, THE RED-NOSED REINDEER: -
DEAN MARTIN
CHRISTMAS WALTZ: - FRANK SINATRA
LET IT SNOW! LET IT SNOW! LET IT
SNOW!: - DEAN MARTIN
HAVE YOURSELF A MERRY LITTLE
CHRISTMAS: - FRANK SINATRA
PEACE ON EARTH / SILENT NIGHT: -
DEAN MARTIN
JINGLE BELLS: - SAMMY DAVIS, JR.
WHITE CHRISTMAS: - DEAN MARTIN
IT CAME UPON A MIDNIGHT CLEAR: -
FRANK SINATRA
WINTER WONDERLAND: - DEAN MARTIN
I'LL BE HOME FOR CHRISTMAS: - FRANK
SINATRA
MARSHMALLOW WORLD: - (WITH AND
DEAN MARTIN) FRANK SINATRA
AULD LANG SYNE: - (WITH AND DEAN
MARTIN) FRANK SINATRA

FRANK SINATRA - RAT PACK: THE EARLY YEARS CD

YOU DO SOMETHING TO ME
IF: - DEAN MARTIN
I AIN'T GOT NOBODY: - SAMMY
DAVIS, JR.
FELLA WITH AN UMBRELLA, A: - PETER
LAWFORD, JUDY GARLAND
SOME ENCHANTED EVENING
SEPTEMBER SONG
IN THE COOL, COOL, COOL OF THE
EVENING: - DEAN MARTIN
I ONLY HAVE EYES FOR YOU
SMILE, DARN YA, SMILE: - SAMMY
DAVIS, JR.
THAT OLD BLACK MAGIC
I'LL ALWAYS LOVE YOU: - DEAN MARTIN
NANCY (WITH THE LAUGHING FACE)
IT'S ONLY A PAPER MOON
DEDICATED TO YOU: - SAMMY
DAVIS, JR.
YOU GO TO MY HEAD
YOU'LL NEVER WALK ALONE
POWDER YOUR FACE WITH SUNSHINE: -
DEAN MARTIN
EMBRACEABLE YOU

OVER THE RAINBOW
WINGIN' WITH RHYTHM AND BLUES: -
JIMMY DURANTE, PETER LAWFORD
NIGHT AND DAY
SATURDAY NIGHT (IS THE LONLIEST
NIGHT OF THE WEEK)
YOU ARE MY LUCKY STAR: - SAMMY
DAVIS, JR.
CONTINENTAL, THE
THESE FOOLISH THINGS
THAT LUCKY OLD SUN: - DEAN MARTIN
WHEN YOU'RE SMILING

BEST OF THE RAT PACK CD - IMPORT

SATURDAY NIGHT (IS THE LONLIEST
NIGHT OF THE WEEK)
EVERYBODY LOVES SOMEBODY: - (WITH
DEAN MARTIN)
WHAT KIND OF FOOL AM I: - (WITH
SAMMY DAVIS, JR.)
THAT OLD BLACK MAGIC: - (WITH
FRANK SINATRA)
WALKIN MY BABY BACK HOME: - (WITH
DEAN MARTIN)

GONNA BUILD A MOUNTAIN: - (WITH SAMMY DAVIS, JR.)
NANCY (WITH THE LAUGHING FACE): - (WITH FRANK SINATRA)
ONCE IN LOVE WITH AMY: - (WITH DEAN MARTIN)
YOURE NOBODY TILL SOMEBODY LOVES YOU: - (WITH SAMMY DAVIS, JR.)
HOW CUTE CAN YOU BE: - (WITH FRANK SINATRA)
DONT LET THE STARS GET IN YOUR EYES: - (WITH DEAN MARTIN)
WITHOUT A SONG: - (WITH SAMMY DAVIS, JR.)
IF I LOVED YOU: - (WITH FRANK SINATRA)
I GOT THE SUN IN THE MORNING: - (WITH DEAN MARTIN)
SOMETHINGS GOTTA GIVE: - (WITH SAMMY DAVIS, JR.)
FIVE MINUTES MORE: - (WITH FRANK SINATRA)
SOME ENCHANTED EVENING: - (WITH DEAN MARTIN)
HEY THERE: - (WITH SAMMY DAVIS, JR.)

BEGINE THE BEGUINE: - (WITH
FRANK SINATRA)
BABY ITS COLD OUTSIDE: - (WITH
DEAN MARTIN)

RAT PACK: 40 TRACKS FROM THE KINGS OF COOL CD - IMPORT

THAT'S AMORE: -(WITH DEAN MARTIN)
WHEN YOU'RE SMILING:- -(WITH FRANK
SINATRA)
YOU'RE NOBODY TILL SOMEBODY LOVES
YOU: - (WITH SAMMY DAVIS, JR.)
MEMORIES ARE MADE OF THIS: - (WITH
DEAN MARTIN)
I'VE GOT A CRUSH ON YOU: - (WITH
FRANK SINATRA)
WITH A SONG IN MY HEART: - (WITH
SAMMY DAVIS, JR.)
EVERYBODY LOVES SOMEBODY: - (WITH
DEAN MARTIN)
BEGIN THE BEGUINE: - (WITH FRANK
SINATRA)
I CAN'T GIVE YOU ANYTHING BUT LOVE:
- (WITH DEAN MARTIN)
ONE FOR MY BABY (AND ONE MORE FOR
THE ROAD): - (WITH FRANK SINATRA)

I'M ALWAYS CHASING RAINBOWS:-
(WITH SAMMY DAVIS, JR.)
BABY IT'S COLD OUTSIDE: - (WITH
DEAN MARTIN)
AUTUMN IN NEW YORK: - (WITH FRANK
SINATRA)
I DON'T CARE IF THE SUN DON'T SHINE:
- (WITH DEAN MARTIN)
BLUE SKIES: - (WITH FRANK SINATRA)
CHICAGO: - (WITH SAMMY DAVIS, JR.)
IF: - (WITH DEAN MARTIN)
BYE BYE BYE: - (WITH FRANK SINATRA)
VOLARE / ON AN EVENING IN ROMA -
DEAN MARTIN: - (WITH DEAN MARTIN)
EVERY TIME WE SAY GOODBYE: - (WITH
SAMMY DAVIS, JR.)
SWAY: - (WITH DEAN MARTIN)
THREE COINS IN THE FOUNTAIN: -
(WITH FRANK SINATRA)
BIRTH OF THE BLUES: - (WITH SAMMY
DAVIS, JR.)
ALL OF ME: - (WITH DEAN MARTIN)
YOUNG AT HEART: - (WITH FRANK
SINATRA)
WHAT KIND OF FOOL AM I: - (WITH
SAMMY DAVIS, JR.)

THAT LUCKY OLD SUN: - (WITH DEAN MARTIN)
THESE FOOLISH THINGS: - (WITH FRANK SINATRA)
I HAVE DREAMED: - (WITH SAMMY DAVIS, JR.)
I WONDER WHO'S KISSING HER NOW: - (WITH DEAN MARTIN)
NIGHT AND DAY: - (WITH FRANK SINATRA)
IMPOSSIBLE DREAM, THE: - (WITH SAMMY DAVIS, JR.)
SEPTEMBER SONG: - (WITH DEAN MARTIN)
WE KISS IN A SHADOW: - (WITH FRANK SINATRA)
ON A CLEAR DAY: - (WITH SAMMY DAVIS, JR.)
WALKIN' MY BABY BACK HOME: - (WITH DEAN MARTIN)
WHERE OR WHEN: - (WITH FRANK SINATRA)
I'VE GOTTA BE ME: - (WITH SAMMY DAVIS, JR.)
ON A SLOW BOAT TO CHINA: - (WITH DEAN MARTIN)

I COULD WRITE A BOOK: - (WITH
FRANK SINATRA)

**FRANK DEAN & SAMMY - RAT PACK
CD - IMPORT**
I ONLY HAVE EYES FOR YOU
PEOPLE WILL SAY WE'RE IN LOVE: -
FRANK SINATRA
ALL OF ME: - DEAN MARTIN
YOU'RE GONNA LOVE YOURSELF: -
SAMMY DAVIS, JR.
OL' MAN RIVER: - FRANK SINATRA
SOMEONE TO WATCH OVER ME: -
FRANK SINATRA
OH MARIE: - DEAN MARTIN
I'LL STRING ALONG WITH YOU: - DEAN
MARTIN
SMOKE, SMOKE, SMOKE: - SAMMY
DAVIS, JR.
WHICH WAY DID MY HEART GO: - DEAN
MARTIN
BEACAUSE YOUR MINE: - DEAN MARTIN
OH, LONESOME ME: - SAMMY
DAVIS, JR.
WE COULD HAVE BEEN THE CLOSEST OF
FRIENDS: - SAMMY DAVIS, JR.

THE SWEATHEART OF SIGMA CHI: -
DEAN MARTIN
OH, WHAT A BEAUTIFUL MORNIN': -
FRANK SINATRA
YOU'LL NEVER WALK ALONE: - FRANK
SINATRA
TILL THEN
ONE FOOT IN HEAVEN: - DEAN MARTIN
SHE'S FUNNY THAT WAY: - FRANK
SINATRA
YOU'LL NEVER KNOW: - FRANK SINATRA
HEY WON'T YOU PLAY(ANOTHER
SOMEBODY DONE SOMEBODY WRONG
SONG)SAMMY DAVIS,JR.
HERE I'LL STAY: - DEAN MARTIN
THE GLOW WORM: - DEAN MARTIN
DAY BY DAY: - FRANK SINATRA
YOU ARE TOO BEAUTIFUL: - FRANK
SINATRA
PLEASE DON'T TELL ME HOW THE
STORY ENDS: - SAMMY DAVIS, JR.
RAMBLING ROSE: - DEAN MARTIN
MEMORY LANE: - DEAN MARTIN
CLOSE TO YOU: - FRANK SINATRA
EMBRACABLE YOU: - FRANK SINATRA
LOUISE: - DEAN MARTIN

THE RIVER'S TOO WIDE: - SAMMY
DAVIS, JR.
WHAT IVE GOT IN MIND: -
HOLD ME: - DEAN MARTIN
MY LADY LOVES TO DANCE: - DEAN
MARTIN
ALL OR NOTHING AT ALL: - FRANK
SINATRA
SATURDAY NIGHT (IS THE LONGEST
NIGHT): - FRANK SINATRA
COME SUNDOWN: - SAMMY DAVIS, JR.
YOU BROUGHT A NEW KIND OF LOVE TO
ME: - FRANK SINATRA
IT'S FUNNY TO EVERYONE BUT ME: -
FRANK SINATRA
SOMEWHERE ALONG THE WAY: - DEAN
MARTIN
IF I KNEW THEN (WHAT I KNOW NOW):
- DEAN MARTIN
DREAM: - FRANK SINATRA
IF I LOVED YOU: - FRANK SINATRA
TAKES TWO TO TANGO: - DEAN MARTIN
ON A SLOW BOAT TO CHINA: - DEAN
MARTIN
MENTION A MANSION: - SAMMY
DAVIS, JR.

I DON'T KONW WHY (I JUST DO): -
FRANK SINATRA

**VARIOUS - RAT PACK AND FRIENDS
CD - IMPORT**
I'VE GOT YOU UNDER MY SKIN: - FRANK
SINATRA
EVERYBODY LOVES SOMEBODY: - DEAN
MARTIN
ALL THE WAY: - FRANK SINATRA
BECAUSE YOU'RE MINE: - DEAN MARTIN
COME FLY WITH ME: - FRANK SINATRA
MY LADY LOVES TO DANCE: - DEAN
MARTIN
YOU MAKE ME FEEL SO YOUNG: - FRANK
SINATRA
RAMBLIN' ROSE: - DEAN MARTIN
WHAT KIND OF FOOL: - SAMMY
DAVIS, JR.
I'LL STRING ALONG WITH YOU: - DEAN
MARTIN
I GET A KICK OUT OF YOU: - FRANK
SINATRA
TAKES TWO TO TANGO: - DEAN MARTIN
MY FUNNY VALENTINE: - FRANK
SINATRA

SOMEWHERE ALONG THE WAY: - DEAN MARTIN
STARDUST: - FRANK SINATRA
O TILL THEN: - DEAN MARTIN
LADY IS A TRAMP: - FRANK SINATRA
OUT OF THIS WORLD: - SAMMY DAVIS, JR.
NIGHT AND DAY: - FRANK SINATRA
HOLD ME: - DEAN MARTIN
BEGIN THE BEGUINE: - FRANK SINATRA
ONE FOOT IN HEAVEN: - DEAN MARTIN
I'VE GOT MY LOVE TO KEEP ME WARM: - FRANK SINATRA
LOUISE: - DEAN MARTIN
LOVE ME OR LEAVE ME: - FRANK SINATRA
MEMORY LANE: - DEAN MARTIN
TEA FOR TWO: - FRANK SINATRA
WHICH WAY DID MY HEART GO: - DEAN MARTIN
AT LONG LAST LOVE: - FRANK SINATRA
ALL OF ME: - DEAN MARTIN
BLUE SKIES: - FRANK SINATRA
I GOT THE SUN IN THE MORNING: - DEAN MARTIN
BEWITCHED: - FRANK SINATRA

SWEETHEART OF SIGNA CHI (GIRL OF MY DREAMS): - DEAN MARTIN
ON THE SUNNY SIDE OF THE STREET: - FRANK SINATRA
OH MARIE: - DEAN MARTIN
EXACTLY LIKE YOU: - SINATRA
MEDLEY: - SINATRA
SOME ENCHANTED EVENING: - SINATRA
PERSONALITY: - SINATRA
TEA FOR TWO: - SINATRA
BEAUTIFUL DREAMER/DE CAMPTOWN RACES: - SINATRA
THIS CAN'T BE LOVE: - SINATRA
MAKE BELIEVE: - SINATRA
FIGARO: - SINATRA
COME OUT WHEREVER YOU ARE: - SINATRA
PARODY MEDLEY: - SINATRA
LOVER COME BACK TO ME: - SINATRA
BIRTH OF THE BLUES: - SINATRA
SOMEBODY LOVES ME: - SINATRA
YOU'D BE SO NICE TO COME HOME TO: - SINATRA
YES INDEED
DON'T BRING LULU: - SINATRA

THERE'S NO BUSINESS LIKE SHOW
BUSINESS: - SINATRA

WELCOME TO THE RAT PACK CD - IMPORT

YOU'RE GONNA LOVE YOURSELF (IN THE
MORNING): - SAMMY DAVIS, JR.
IF I LOVED YOU: - FRANK SINATRA
MACARTHUR PARK: - SAMMY
DAVIS, JR.
CANDY KISSES: - DEAN MARTIN
LOVELY WAY TO SPEND AN EVENING: -
FRANK SINATRA
WHAT I'VE GOT IN MIND: - SAMMY
DAVIS, JR.
TAKE YOUR GIRL TO THE MOVIES: -
DEAN MARTIN
NANCY (WITH THE LAUGHING FACE): -
FRANK SINATRA
HEY WON'T YOU PLAY(ANOTHER
SOMEBODY DONE SOMEBODY WRONG
SONG)SAMMY DAVIS,JR.
RIDERS IN THE SKY: - DEAN MARTIN
I'LL BE SEEING YOU: - FRANK SINATRA
MENTION A MANSION: - SAMMY
DAVIS, JR.

SWANNEE: - DEAN MARTIN
I CAN'T GIVE YOU ANYTHING BUT LOVE:
- DEAN MARTIN
IN THE BLUE OF THE EVENING: - FRANK
SINATRA
SMOKE SMOKE SMOKE (THAT
CIGARETTE):-SAMMY DAVIS, JR.

**RAT PACK: LIVE & COOL DEAN
MARTIN AND SAMMY DAVIS JR.**
MEDLEY: WHEN YOU'RE SMILING/THE
LADY IS A TRAMP - THE RAT PACK,
FISHER
I LEFT MY HEART IN SAN FRANCISCO -
THE RAT PACK, CORY, GEORGE
I'M GONNA SIT RIGHT DOWN AND
WRITE MYSELF A LETTER - THE RAT
PACK, AHLERT, FRED E.
MEDLEY: VOLARE/ON AN EVENING WITH
ROMA - THE RAT PACK, BERTINI
GOODY, GOODY - THE RAT PACK,
MALNECK, MATTY
CHICAGO - THE RAT PACK, FISHER,
FRED
WHEN YOUR LOVER HAS GONE - THE
RAT PACK, SWAN, EINAR A.

PLEASE BE KIND - THE RAT PACK, CAHN, SAMMY

YOU'RE NOBODY 'TIL SOMEBODY LOVES YOU - THE RAT PACK, CAVANAUGH, JAMES

WHAT KIND OF FOOL AM I - THE RAT PACK, BRICUSSE

OUT OF THIS WORLD - THE RAT PACK, ARLEN, HAROLD

HEY THERE - THE RAT PACK, ADLER, RICHARD [COM]

I CAN'T GIVE YOU ANYTHING BUT LOVE - THE RAT PACK, FIELDS, DOROTHY

TOO MARVELLOUS FOR WORDS - THE RAT PACK, MERCER

PENNIES FROM HEAVEN - THE RAT PACK, BURKE, JOHNNY

A FOGGY DAY - THE RAT PACK, GERSHWIN, GEORGE

ME & MY SHADOW - THE RAT PACK, DREYER, DAVE

JUNE IN JANUARY - THE RAT PACK, MARTIN

VIA VENETO - THE RAT PACK, SCHWAB

UNKNOWN FORMAT 2: RAT PACK- LIVE & COOL

I ONLY HAVE EYES FOR YOU - THE RAT PACK, DUBIN, AL

MY HEART STOOD STILL - THE RAT PACK, RODGERS, RICHARD

PLEASE BE KIND - THE RAT PACK, CAHN, SAMMY

CALL ME IRRESPONSIBLE - THE RAT PACK, CAHN, SAMMY

LUCKY BE A LADY - THE RAT PACK, LOESSER, FRANK

THE LADY IS A TRAMP - THE RAT PACK, LOESSER

ROCK-A-BYE-YOUR-BABY - THE RAT PACK, LEWIS

GUYS & DOLLS - THE RAT PACK, LOESSER, FRANK

CRAP GRAP IN NEW YORK - THE RAT PACK, LOESSER, FRANK

SEND ME THE PILLOW THAT YOU DREAM ON - THE RAT PACK, LOCKLIN, HANK

KING OF THE ROAD - THE RAT PACK, MILLER

EVERYBODY LOVES SOMEBODY - THE
RAT PACK, LANE, BURTON
MY SHINING HOUR - THE RAT PACK,
ARLEN, HAROLD
WHO CAN I TURN TO (WHEN NOBODY
NEEDS ME) - THE RAT PACK, BRICUSSE,
LESLIE
FLY ME TO THE MOON - THE RAT PACK,
HOWARD
I'VE GOT YOU UNDER MY SKIN - THE
RAT PACK, PORTER, COLE
YOU MAKE ME FEEL SO YOUNG - THE
RAT PACK, GORDON
MY KIND OF TOWN - THE RAT PACK,
CAHN, SAMMY
BIRTH OF THE BLUES/CLOSING TUNE -
THE RAT PACK, BROWN, LEW

RATPACK-VEGAS TO ST. LOUIS
DEAN'S VEGAS MELODY - THE RAT PACK,
(NOT USED IN STORY)
MONOLOGUE - THE RAT PACK,
JUNE IN JANUARY - THE RAT PACK,
RAINGER, RALPH
VIA VENETO - THE RAT PACK,
SCHWABB, MARTIN

VOLARE - THE RAT PACK, MIGLIACCI,
FRANCESC
ON AN EVENING IN ROMA (SOTT'ER
CELO DE ROMA) - THE RAT PACK,
BERINI
I ONLY HAVE EYES FOR YOU - THE RAT
PACK, DUBIN, AL
MY HEART STOOD STILL - THE RAT
PACK, HART, LORENZ
PLEASE BE KIND - THE RAT PACK, CAHN,
SAMMY
MONOLOGUE - THE RAT PACK,
CALL ME IRRESPONSIBLE - THE RAT
PACK, CAHN, SAMMY
LUCK BE A LADY - THE RAT PACK,
LOESSER, FRANK
AT THE 'SALAD BAR' - THE RAT PACK,
KIDDIE ALBUM MEDLEY - THE RAT PACK,
SAMMY DAVIS JR. - THE RAT PACK,
THE LADY IS A TRAMP - THE RAT PACK,
HART, LORENZ
ROCK-A-BYE YOUR BABY - THE RAT
PACK, LEWIS, SAM M.
SAMMY'S MARCH - THE RAT PACK,
GUYS AND DOLLS - THE RAT PACK,
LOESSER, FRANK

CRAP GAME IN NEW YORK - THE RAT
PACK, LOESSER, FRANK
ENCORE - THE RAT PACK,
INSTRUMENTAL - THE RAT PACK,

UNKNOWN FORMAT 2 : RATPACK-VEGAS TO ST. LOUIS

JOHNNY CARSON INTRODUCES DEAN
MARTIN - THE RAT PACK, (NOT USED IN
STORY)
SEND ME THE PILLOW YOU DREAM ON -
THE RAT PACK, LOCKLIN, HANK
KING OF THE ROAD - THE RAT PACK,
MILLER, ROGER [COUN
EVERYBODY LOVES SOMEBODY - THE
RAT PACK, COSLOW, SAM
MEDLEY: VOLARE/ON AN EVENING WITH
ROMA - THE RAT PACK, BERTINI,
UMBERTO
JOHNNY CARSON INTRODUCES SAMMY
DAVIS JR. - THE RAT PACK, (NOT USED
IN STORY)
MY SHINING HOUR - THE RAT PACK,
ARLEN, HAROLD
MONOLOGUE - THE RAT PACK,

WHO CAN I TURN TO (WHEN NOBODY NEEDS ME) - THE RAT PACK, BRICUSSEL

MEDLEY: I'VE GOT YOU UNDER MY SKIN/YOU ARE MY SUNSHINE - THE RAT PACK, PORTER, COLE

ONE FOR MY BABY (AND ONE MORE FOR THE ROAD) - THE RAT PACK, ARLEN, HAROLD

JOHNNY CARSON INTRODUCES FRANK SINATRA - THE RAT PACK, (NOT USED IN STORY)

GET ME TO THE CHURCH ON TIME - THE RAT PACK, LERNER, ALAN JAY

FLY ME TO THE MOON - THE RAT PACK, HOWARD, BART

LUCK BE A LADY - THE RAT PACK, LOESSER, FRANK

I ONLY HAVE EYES FOR YOU - THE RAT PACK, DUBIN, AL

I'VE GOT YOU UNDER MY SKIN - THE RAT PACK, PORTER, COLE

MONOLOGUE - THE RAT PACK,

PLEASE BE KIND - THE RAT PACK, CAHN, SAMMY

YOU MAKE ME FEEL SO YOUNG - THE
RAT PACK, GORDON, MACK
MY KIND OF TOWN - THE RAT PACK,
CAHN, SAMMY
RATPACK MONOLOGUE - THE RAT PACK,
(NOT USED IN STORY)
BIRTH OF THE BLUES (CLOSING TUNE) -
THE RAT PACK, BROW

BIBLIOGRAPHY

VERY BEST OF THE RAT PACK CD:
http://www.cduniverse.com/productinfo.a
sp?pid=8311103

RAT PACK CD:
http://www.cduniverse.com/productinfo.a
sp?pid=7508233&style=classical

50 ORIGINAL RECORDINGS CD –
IMPORT:
http://www.cduniverse.com/productinfo.a
sp?pid=7447713&style=classical

STARS THAT MADE LOS VEGAS CD –
IMPORT:
http://www.cduniverse.com/productinfo.a
sp?pid=6706142&style=classical

ON THE SUNNY SIDE OF THE STREET CD
– IMPORT:
http://www.cduniverse.com/productinfo.a
sp?pid=1455899&style=classical

ULTIMATE COLLECTION CD – IMPORT:
http://www.cduniverse.com/productinfo.a
sp?pid=7527149&style=classical

RAT PACK-THE BIG THREE CD –
IMPORT:
http://www.cduniverse.com/productinfo.a
sp?pid=7755576&style=classical

RAT PACK - ALWAYS CD – IMPORT:
http://www.cduniverse.com/productinfo.a
sp?pid=7541166

LEGENDARY RAT PACK CD – IMPORT:
http://www.cduniverse.com/productinfo.a
sp?pid=7026740&style=classical

RAKISH & RAMPANT CD:
http://www.cduniverse.com/productinfo.a
sp?pid=7516429&style=classical

STARS IN LAS VEGAS: 200 FAMOUS
TRACKS CD:
http://www.cduniverse.com/productinfo.a
sp?pid=6802683

RAT PACK - BOY'S NIGHT OUT CD:
http://www.cduniverse.com/productinfo.a
sp?pid=6778627

RAT PACK - SEPTEMBER SONG CD:
http://www.cduniverse.com/productinfo.a
sp?pid=6881640

RAT PACK - BEST OF CD – IMPORT:
http://www.cduniverse.com/productinfo.a
sp?pid=7274532

RAT PACK - ON STAGE CD – IMPORT:
http://www.cduniverse.com/productinfo.a
sp?pid=6787938

VERY BEST OF CD – IMPORT:
http://www.cduniverse.com/productinfo.a
sp?pid=7293386&style=classical

ULTIMATE RATPACK CD – IMPORT:
http://www.cduniverse.com/productinfo.a
sp?pid=7413786&style=classical

FAR AWAY PLACES CD – IMPORT:
http://www.cduniverse.com/productinfo.a
sp?pid=7397356&style=classical

RAT PACK - DEAN MARTIN FRANK
SINATRA SAMMY DAVIS CD – IMPORT:
http://www.cduniverse.com/productinfo.a
sp?pid=7328054

FRANK SINATRA-DEAN MARTIN CD –
IMPORT:
http://www.cduniverse.com/productinfo.a
sp?pid=7320205&style=classical

RAT PACK VOL. 3-THE RAT PACK CD –
IMPORT:
http://www.cduniverse.com/productinfo.a
sp?pid=7318494

TRIBUTE TO RAT PACK : TRIBUTE TO
THE RAT PACK VOL. 2-TRIBUTE TO THE
RAT PACK CD:
http://www.cduniverse.com/productinfo.a
sp?pid=7310751

TRIBUTE TO RAT PACK : TRIBUTE TO
THE RAT PACK VOL. 1-TRIBUTE TO THE
RAT PACK CD:
http://www.cduniverse.com/productinfo.a
sp?pid=7310750

LIVE AND SWINGIN' : THE RAT PACK
LIVE AT THE VILLA VENICE DVD AUDIO:
http://www.cduniverse.com/productinfo.a
sp?pid=6376908

BEST OF THE RAT PACK VOL. 1 MP3
ALBUM:
http://www.cduniverse.com/mp3search.a
sp?ht_search_info=11821123&ht_search
=mp3album&style=mp3

BEST OF THE RAT PACK VOL. 2 MP3
ALBUM:
http://www.cduniverse.com/mp3search.a
sp?ht_search_info=11821124&ht_search
=mp3album&style=mp3

SAMMY DAVIS, JR / DEAN MARTIN /
FRANK SINATRA - LIVE AND SWINGIN':
THE ULTIMATE RAT PACK COLLECTION
CD:
http://www.cduniverse.com/productinfo.a
sp?pid=6329829&cart=1160502493

TRIBUTE TO RAT PACK : TRIBUTE TO
THE RAT PACK VOL. 3-TRIBUTE TO THE
RAT PACK CD:
http://www.cduniverse.com/productinfo.a
sp?pid=7310752

FRANK SINATRA - CHRISTMAS WITH
THE RAT PACK AND FRIENDS CD:
http://www.cduniverse.com/productinfo.a
sp?pid=7116457

DEAN MARTIN - CHRISTMAS WITH THE
RAT PACK CD:
http://www.cduniverse.com/productinfo.a
sp?pid=8247633

CHRISTMAS WITH THE RAT PACK MP3
ALBUM:
http://www.cduniverse.com/mp3search.a
sp?ht_search_info=9675771&ht_search=
mp3album&style=mp3

FRANK SINATRA - RAT PACK: THE EARLY
YEARS CD:
http://www.cduniverse.com/productinfo.a
sp?pid=4891170

BEST OF THE RAT PACK CD – IMPORT:
http://www.cduniverse.com/productinfo.a
sp?pid=5358306

RAT PACK: 40 TRACKS FROM THE KINGS
OF COOL CD – IMPORT:
http://www.cduniverse.com/productinfo.a
sp?pid=6865920

RAT PACK: LIVE & COOL DEAN MARTIN
AND SAMMY DAVIS JR.: rat pack: live &
cool dean martin and sammy davis jr. &
unknown format 2 : rat pack-live &
cool:http://www.soundunwound.com/mu
sic/dean-martin/rat-pack-live-and-
cool/12110177?ref=di

FRANK DEAN & SAMMY - RAT PACK CD –
IMPORT:
http://www.cduniverse.com/productinfo.a
sp?pid=7027816

VARIOUS - RAT PACK AND FRIENDS CD
– IMPORT:
http://www.cduniverse.com/productinfo.a
sp?pid=7268938

WELCOME TO THE RAT PACK CD –
IMPORT:
http://www.cduniverse.com/productinfo.a
sp?pid=7451798

RATPACK-VEGAS TO ST. LOUIS:
http://www.soundunwound.com/music/d
ean-martin/ratpack-vegas-to-st-
louis/13899601?ref=di

ABOUT THE AUTHOR

I was 59 years old; a mother of three very special and supportive adult children and a grandmother of three wonderful grandsons (I now have five grand-children.) when I started writing my first book whilst watching a Bon Jovi concert DVD. (I am an avid fan, if you can call me that; crazy is more like it.)

I write from the heart and I really enjoyed writing the book so I wrote another using a different artist, and the books kept coming to me and I kept writing them.(with a little help from above)

Because I use different artist/artists song titles I have to be very careful with Copyright so a lot of legal requirements have to be taken into consideration before publishing the books. I also needed a name that would connect my books to each other; so the "Song Title Series" books began.

All my books are short stories; however it depends on how many song titles there are to be used, as to the length of the book. Some artists didn't have enough song titles on their own so I combined them with a few other artists. Other artists had that many song titles that I could have written a novel; but it would have ended up being boring.

Challenges I like, so writing books with various artists are a lot of fun and require careful thinking.

Why should I have all the fun writing the books and not be able to share them with everyone; so I have converted them into large print books so that you can share my fun as well.

Hopefully in the not too distant future; the books will also be available as audio books so that no-one will miss out on my fun and enjoyment of writing these unique books. I hope that you enjoy reading them.

My web site www.songtitleseries.com is the place to visit for updates of new books and a place to purchase other titles in other formats.

OTHER BOOKS IN THE
SONG TITLE SERIES

Bon Jovi – Wanted Dead Or Alive
Green Day
AC/DC
Beach Boys
Slim Dusty
Country Women
Five Country Men
Six Crooners
Three Crooners
ABBA
The Rat Pack
Elton John
Classic 50s & 60s Rock 'N' Roll

TESTIMONIALS

I am Susie and would like to tell you guys, how much I am enjoying Joan Maguire's Books!! They are very enjoyable, and they are something that you do not ever want to put down!! I really enjoy these books; I can't wait until the next one that she puts out!!!!!!! I say go to your local book store, today and get one, you will not be disappointed!!!!!
Sue-from the United States of America

The song titles series are books that were intriguing and were hard to believe that these short stories were written within the incorporated song titles of the artists that are mentioned in the titles. I loved what I have read so far and think that anyone with an imagination and love of music as the author you will surely enjoy reading these.
L.K. Brisbane Australia.

Joan Maguire Books are very nice, I enjoy reading them so much, they are hard to put down!! Especially when she does one about Bonjovi and their songs!!!

If I can say, it is worth every penny, when you buy one!!! The Books make nice presents, for a person whom loves to read!!! I can guarantee that you will LOVE these books, because I do!!!!!!!!! Dawn from Newark, Delaware in the United States of America

After reading through your range of books I felt I must compliment you Joan on the imaginative and entertaining way in which you presented each group and the Musicians in those groups. The way the stories were constructed is a credit to your work ethic. These must have taken considerable time to piece together and it is obviously a work of love for you.
I wish you all the success you truly deserve and look forward to seeing you next time you visit Tamworth.
Peter Harkins   Managing Director Cheapa Music   Country Music Capital Tamworth

---